Dear Brio Girl,

Becca definitely wants to be the hands and feet of Jesus to those around her. And that's a good thing, right? After all, God is counting on His followers to change the world, spread the gospel and love unconditionally. But is there ever a point that a Christian can be too involved with good things? Join Becca in a dangerous struggle to find balance while being obedient in Going Crazy Till Wednesday.

Your Friend,

Susie Shellenberger, BRIO Editor
www.briomag.com

BRIO GIRLS®

from Focus on the Family®
and
Tyndale House Publishers, Inc.

REAL Faith MEETS REAL Life sm

Jacie   Hannah   Solana   Tyler

Going Crazy
Till Wednesday

Created by

LISSA HALLS JOHNSON

WRITTEN BY JANE VOGEL

TYNDALE

Tyndale House Publishers, inc.
Wheaton, Illinois

Going Crazy Till Wednesday
Copyright © 2003, Focus on the Family. All rights reserved.

A Focus on the Family book published by
Tyndale House Publishers, Inc., Wheaton, Illinois 60189; First printing, 2005
Previously published by Bethany House under the same ISBN.

Tyndale's quill logo is a trademark of Tyndale House Publishers, Inc.
BRIO GIRLS is a registered trademark of Focus on the Family.

Cover design by Lookout Design Group, Inc.
Editor: Lissa Halls Johnson

This story is a work of fiction. With the exception of recognized historical figures, the characters are the product of the author's imagination. Any resemblance to any person, living or dead, is coincidental.

Library of Congress Cataloging-in-Publication Data

Vogel, Jane.
   Going crazy till Wednesday / created by Lissa Halls Johnson ; written by Jane Vogel.— 1st ed.
      p. cm. — (Brio girls)
   "A Focus on the Family book."
   Summary: Now a senior in high school, Becca is consumed by plans to organize an outdoor adventure program for children at the shelter where she volunteers, but a fire destroys their supplies before the program can begin.
   ISBN 1-58997-089-6
   [1. Camping—Fiction. 2. Shelters for the homeless—Fiction. 3. Christian life—Fiction. 4. High schools—Fiction. 5. Schools—Fiction.] I. Johnson, Lissa Halls, 1955- II. Title. III. Series.

   PZ7.V8672Go 2003
[Fic]—dc22   2003020745

Printed in the United States of America

11 10 09 08 07 06 05
9 8 7 6 5 4 3 2 1

For Theresa,
who provided the initial "spark" for this book,
and for the WCRC Summer Bible Study 2003 members,
who prayed me through all the times
I was going crazy till deadlines.

JANE VOGEL is a perpetually over-committed writer and youth worker in Wheaton, Illinois, where she lives with her husband, two children, one guinea pig, two goldfish, and three hamsters (at last count).

chapter 1

"One week left of vacation," Becca McKinnon sang out, knocking out a percussion accompaniment on her sister Kassy's bedroom door. A muffled groan was the only response. Becca grinned as she bounded down the stairs to the kitchen. Kassy's idea of making the most of vacation was to sleep in. Becca, on the other hand, figured time was wasted if she wasn't moving in fast motion.

"'Morning, Mom! 'Morning, Alvaro!" she said, pausing to drop a kiss on her little brother's shiny black hair as she passed the kitchen table. "Got any bagels? I've got to eat breakfast on the run today."

"What else is new?" her mother said, with a glance at the clock on the stove. "If you'd get up more than five minutes before you have to leave, you could actually sit down for a meal for once. And maybe even brush your hair," she added as an afterthought, with a resigned look at the ponytail Becca had hastily pulled her tangled brown hair into as she ran down the stairs.

"I sit down for supper almost every night, thanks to my old-fashioned parents who think families have to eat together," Becca teased as she grabbed a bagel from the counter and rummaged in the fridge for cream cheese. "And my hair will just get messy as soon as I start playing with the kids at the Community Center anyway."

"Oh! That reminds me," said her mother. "Mrs. Robeson called before you got up. She wants to see you when you get to the Center."

"I'm not in trouble, am I?" Becca asked warily. Mrs. Robeson, the Community Center director, was more than a little formidable. She seemed to be able to be everywhere and know everything, and more than once Becca's impulsiveness had earned her a reprimand from Mrs. Robeson.

"I don't think so," Mrs. McKinnon replied. "She said she wanted to talk with you about taking on more responsibility."

"Maybe she wants to upgrade me from volunteer to paid status," Becca said hopefully. "Think so?"

"Not likely," Mrs. McKinnon said dryly. "We can't pay the staff we have what they deserve, much less add on."

Becca made a wry face, but she just shrugged. Her mom, as a part-time administrator at the Community Center, knew how tight finances were for the Christian organization. If she said there was no money, Becca believed her. It didn't matter; Becca volunteered in the Community Center's recreation program and at the Center's homeless shelter because she wanted to help make a difference, not because she ever thought she'd make any money off it.

"Probably Mrs. R. just wants to know what my volunteer schedule will be once school starts," she said, slathering her bagel with cream cheese. She crammed the bagel into her mouth to free her hands so she could open the glass-fronted key case that hung by the side door. "Can I borrow your keys, Mom?" she asked around the bagel, unhooking a set of keys without waiting for an answer. "I can't find mine."

"And Mrs. Robeson wants to give you *more* responsibility?" Becca's mother said with a lift of her eyebrows.

Ignoring the comment, Becca headed out the door. "Bye, Mom!

Bye, Alvaro!" she said with a wave of her bagel. "Gotta run!"

● ● ●

"'Morning, Angela," Becca said to the receptionist in the lobby of Outreach Community Center. "Can you please get me the volunteer sheet? I need to sign in."

"Why, sure, Honey," the older woman said, pulling a black notebook out of a drawer and setting it on the counter with a ballpoint pen. "Why are you here? This isn't one of your usual days."

"Keeping track of me, are you?" teased Becca. "If I ever need an alibi, I'll tell the cops to come to you. You can give them my whole schedule."

"Yours and most everybody who comes here," Angela said matter-of-factly. "That's part of my job—to know what's going on here. You, now—you come one Saturday a month regular when you're in school, plus sometimes an extra afternoon after school. Summertime you come every Saturday." She looked at Becca over her half-glasses. "Excepting last Saturday you didn't come at all, and now here you are on a Monday." She crossed her arms over her substantial bosom and waited, clearly expecting an explanation.

"I know—my schedule's all messed up," Becca said with a smile. "I took last Saturday off to spend at my friend's ranch—it was a kind of celebration. And I can't be here the next two Saturdays either. My brother Matt is going back to college next week, so my family is going to spend Saturday together. And I'll be gone the next weekend to a leadership retreat for the Edge. You know—the youth ministry that meets at Stony Brook High School. So I'm putting in some time during the week to help out instead."

"There now—I knew there'd be a reason for it," Angela said. "I just like to keep track of people, that's all."

"You're the best at it," Becca assured her.

"Most every time, I am—but I'm still fretting about that time your missing friend called and I didn't get his number." Angela shook her

·head slowly. "That was just too bad. You hear from him yet?"

"Otis? Nope." Becca signed her name and noted her arrival time in the volunteer notebook and pushed it over the counter to Angela. "Are you still worrying about that? That was months ago."

"Parachuting friend of yours, wasn't he?" Angela recalled. "He got himself in some parachuting accident and got hauled off to the hospital who-knows-where, and you haven't heard from him since."

"Paragliding," Becca corrected. "Not parachuting. He crashed and had to be lifted out by helicopter, so I never got to talk to him or the rescue team. I didn't even know if he was alive till he called here and left that message."

"Funny kind of message, too, wasn't it?" Angela said. "I don't rightly recall it just now, but seems to me it didn't make sense."

"He said to tell me he's okay, to keep praying, that he met a friend of mine, and that he'd be back in the harness when he gets the casts off." Becca repeated the message from memory. She'd read it over and over after Angela had given it to her last spring, hoping to find some clue about how to reach Otis. But he hadn't left a number, and Becca didn't know his last name from their casual friendship paragliding together. Finally she had to be satisfied with posting the message on her bedroom bulletin board and using it as a reminder to pray for Otis.

"That's right," Angela chuckled. "Back in the harness—that's what struck me funny. Sounds like an old pack mule."

Becca smiled at the thought of Otis as a pack mule, plodding along some boring track carrying a load for someone else. Nothing could be further from the Otis she knew: He seemed to like adventure as much as Becca did herself.

"Otis *is* older, I guess," she told Angela. "Maybe 30—I'm not sure." She grinned as Angela shook her head at the description of 30 as old. "But he's no pack mule. The harness is what you hook your paragliding wing to," she explained. She paused, thinking over the message. "What struck *me* funny was him asking me to pray for him."

"Now, Honey, you surprise me!" Angela said. "I would've thought you were for sure a praying girl."

"Oh, I am!" Becca assured her. "But Otis isn't. A praying guy, I mean. He's not even a Christian."

"Well then, you best do the praying for both you *and* him," Angela said. "You and that friend of yours he said he met."

"That's the other funny thing," Becca said slowly. "I never did figure out who he met. None of my friends from school know him, and every time I go paragliding I ask whoever's there, but nobody else has run into him either."

"Just a mystery, isn't it?" Angela shifted her weight and resettled herself into her chair. "Well, I reckon the Lord will sort it out for you one of these days. He most always does. Meanwhile, I'll be sure to get that Otis's number for you if he ever calls again."

"Thanks, Angela! I hope he does." Becca impulsively leaned over the counter to give Angela a hug before heading down the hall to check in with Mrs. Robeson.

Mrs. Robeson's office was, as usual, as neat and organized as Mrs. Robeson herself. Her desk and filing cabinets were a good deal more battered than Angela's receptionist station—Becca knew from her mom's work on the Community Center budget that Mrs. Robeson regularly redirected any money budgeted for her office to other areas that more directly affected the clients. But the file folders stacked in the "to do" basket were crisp and cleanly labeled. Becca noted that the basket of work completed and ready to be refiled was stacked higher than the "to do" basket. Glancing at her watch, she marveled at Mrs. Robeson's efficiency. *It's only 9:30 on Monday morning. How does she manage to get so much done?* Becca wondered. *Especially when it seems like she's never in her office.*

For, as usual, the chair behind the desk was empty. *Mrs. R. must be out making the rounds of the Center again,* Becca decided. Mrs. Robeson's quiet inspections were just part of the routine to the staff and regular volunteers, but Becca knew how unnerving it could be to a new volunteer to turn around and discover that Mrs. Robeson had been quietly observing for who-knows-how-long!

Leaving Mrs. Robeson's office, Becca peeked into the library across the hall. *Nope—not there.* She walked down the west wing hallway and stuck her head through one of the doorways into the homeless shelter in the northwest corner of the building. Shelter rules required clients to be up and out by 8:00 A.M.; adults were supposed to be out job-hunting or in one of the life-skills classes the Community Center offered, and kids attended summer school and recreation sessions. So Becca wasn't surprised to find the women and children's room empty except for the small stacks of personal belongings separating the mattresses laid out on the floor.

"Mrs. R.?" she called, in case Mrs. Robeson was on the other side of the accordion-pleated divider that screened off this section from the men's sleeping area. No one answered, and Becca decided against picking her way through the rows of mattresses to check in person. The floor looked even more crowded than she remembered from two weeks before, when she had helped serve Saturday breakfast at the shelter. Automatically she did a quick bed count. *Twenty-seven.* Becca shook her head. Technically the women's side was supposed to hold only 24 mattresses so as to allow enough clear aisleway to satisfy the fire marshal. Becca knew Mrs. Robeson would never violate the fire code, so she must have figured out some way to squeeze in the extra mattresses without blocking access to the emergency exit.

Running her eye along the rows of mattresses again, Becca realized how they'd done it: Several women had given up their precious inches of "personal" space for their belongings. Instead of having a few inches between mattresses, some of the bedding was pressed side by side. *How hard is it to sleep with people pushed up right next to you like that?* Becca wondered. *I thought it was a squeeze getting our whole family in our tent this summer when we went camping, and that was just for a week. Here maybe a dozen families are all crowded together.* She felt a flash of anger at the Copper Ridge city zoning board. Becca's mom had petitioned for approval to expand the shelter, but the board kept dragging their feet on the decision. *I'd like to see them sleep here for a week*, Becca thought. *Maybe then they'd see how much we need more space!*

A thudding from the kitchen attracted her attention, and she walked down the hall to see who was there. André, one of the recreation program leaders, was hoisting five-gallon thermal jugs onto the counter that opened onto the gym and setting them down with a thump.

"Hey, Becca!" he said as Becca stuck her head into the kitchen. He motioned to the jugs. "It's going to be a hot one today. The kids'll need plenty to drink." André stretched a long arm to flip open a cabinet and easily reached an industrial-sized box of paper cups on the top shelf. "You helping out in the rec program today?"

"Probably," Becca said. "I'm supposed to check in with Mrs. R. first. Have you seen her?"

"Not yet. But the first rec session isn't until 10. She usually comes in here around then." André looked at his watch. "She's probably over in the classrooms right now."

Becca nodded. "Thanks, André. I'll try to be back to help out by the time the first group comes in."

Becca cut through the empty gym and headed over to the east wing of the Community Center. Here a large multiclassroom space housed the more academic aspects of the summer program for school-aged kids. Portable dividers separated age groups. Like just about everything else at Outreach Community Center, the room was filled to capacity. Mrs. Robeson, her ever-present clipboard in hand, was observing the remedial reading teacher as she coached a small group of children on long vowel sounds.

"Mrs. R.," Becca said in a low voice, so as not to distract the kids.

Mrs. Robeson nodded, made a note on her clipboard, then motioned Becca to follow her out of the classroom. She led the way to the corner stairwell.

"Mom said you wanted to talk to me," Becca said, mounting the stairs behind Mrs. Robeson.

"Yes, I do, Becca!" Mrs. Robeson stopped on the stairs and smiled at Becca. "I've been thinking for some time now that you're ready for more responsibility here, and now I have a real need that I think you can help meet."

Becca beamed with pleasure. Mrs. Robeson's standards could be demanding, and a word of praise from her meant as much as an award from someone else. She met Mrs. Robeson's eyes and tried hard not to look like the kind of person who would lose her keys.

"Where I really need you is on the night shift at the homeless shelter. One of our regular volunteers moved away, and I've been short-staffed ever since." She looked at Becca. "The problem is that you're only 17."

Becca felt the familiar surge of frustration she always got when an adult implied that being young was a "problem." "Yes, I'm *already* 17," she replied, "and I'm starting my senior year in high school next week. Plus I've been volunteering at the homeless shelter for . . . well, ages," she concluded lamely, wishing she could rattle off the exact amount of time she had been a volunteer as efficiently as Mrs. Robeson could recall the ages of her volunteers.

"Your experience isn't the problem, Becca," Mrs. Robeson explained patiently. "I wouldn't be asking you if I didn't think you were qualified. The problem is that we need someone 21 or older on every shift for insurance reasons." Mrs. Robeson ran her pencil down a calendar print-out on the clipboard. "Gordon would be a perfect partner for you. He works a full-time job, so he can be on call here, but he needs to sleep. You could take responsibility for whatever minor things arise during the night, and Gordon would be your backup in an emergency." Transferring her gaze from the clipboard to Becca, she asked, "Do you think you could handle that? It would be a weekend night of course—not a school night."

"I know I could!" Becca said immediately. "I know practically all the clients already, from volunteering on the breakfast shift. And of course I know the kids from the rec program. I could do it, Mrs. R."

"It's not your ability I'm asking about, it's the time commitment," Mrs. Robeson said. "Taking on a night shift is a big commitment, and I assume you have other responsibilities at home and school."

Becca nodded. As usual, she had answered impulsively, without thinking through all the implications. She pressed her fist to her mouth as she forced herself to slow her thoughts and assess whether she really did think she could handle an all-night shift. Mrs. Robeson deserved a serious response to her question.

"Schoolwork shouldn't be a problem," she said finally. "I could always take that along and work on it here, right? And Mom and Dad don't expect me to work a paying job during the school year, so that's okay. The only problem," she admitted, "is during basketball season. If I have a Friday night game, I could cover the Saturday night shift at the shelter, but if the game is on Saturday, I know Coach won't want me staying up all night Friday."

Mrs. Robeson nodded. "I understand. We'd have some things to work out. When does basketball season start?"

"Practice starts at the end of October, but games don't start until the end of November."

"That gives us a little time to come up with some solutions," Mrs. Robeson said. "In the meantime, if you think you'd like to try this, I want you to talk with your parents and get their permission as well."

"Okay," Becca agreed. She really liked it that Mrs. Robeson talked with her about the night shift first, instead of getting her parents' approval before talking to Becca. *I guess Mrs. R. really doesn't see being young as a problem*, she decided. *She treats me with the same respect she gives the adults*. Becca resolved to prove that she was worthy of that respect.

Walking briskly to a classroom door, Mrs. Robeson said over her shoulder, "Today's the new middle-school teacher's first day on the job. I was going to help him take the class down to the gym, but since you're going there next, why don't you show him the way?"

"Sure," Becca said. "But the kids could show him the way just as well."

Mrs. Robeson turned the doorknob to the classroom. "They could," she agreed. "But I have some doubt that they *would*." She opened the door and entered the middle-school room. "Oh, dear," Becca heard her say. "Oh, dear!"

chapter

"You the man, Ricky!"

A Babel of confused shouts came through the open door of the middle-school classroom, and Becca, curious to know what was going on, followed closely behind Mrs. Robeson as she strode into the room.

A group of 11 or 12 kids crowded around one of the desks, girls in one clump and boys in another. Standing on the desk in the center of the group was Ricky Williams, one of the seventh-grade boys Becca knew from the rec program. He waved a small purple, fur-covered book above his head.

"I've got Gina's di-a-ry, I've got Gina's di-a-ry," he singsonged.

"Give it back," shrieked a girl with wavy brown hair and neon green fingernails. Becca didn't recognize her, but from the way she clambered up onto the desk and clawed at Ricky, Becca figured the girl must be Gina, the owner of the diary. "Give it back, or you'll be sorry!"

"Ooh!" chorused the crowd of boys. "Hear that, Ricky? Gina's gonna make you sorry!"

As was typical, Mrs. Robeson stood back, waiting for the teacher to take control of the situation.

Furiously the girl kicked at the boys, but they jumped out of reach, and the wild movement threw her off balance just long enough for Ricky to lower the diary to eye level and open it.

"Dear Diary," he cooed in a high-pitched imitation of a girl's voice, but the outraged cries of the girls drowned him out. Gina made another grab for the diary, and Ricky quickly raised it above his head again.

A shout of "Ricky—over here!" drew Becca's attention to the other side of the room. Guillermo, another of the seventh-grade boys, raised his arms as if to receive a pass, and Ricky hurled the diary to him. With a mad rush, the girls charged Guillermo, kicking over chairs and shoving desks out of their way. But just before they reached him, he threw the diary back to Ricky. The other boys stamped their feet and cheered their approval, while the girls, furious at being forced into a game of "monkey in the middle," screamed insults at the boys.

Where is the new teacher? Becca wondered. *And why isn't he putting a stop to this?* A quick glance to the front of the room revealed a pale young man with very bad skin nervously clenching and unclenching his hands. *Come to think of it, why hasn't Mrs. Robeson done something by now?*

"Okay, class," he finally called out in a tentative voice. "That's enough." He hesitated a moment then wove his way through the clutter of scattered desks and chairs. "Okay, ahh . . . Ricky," he said. He cleared his throat and held out a hand. "Uh, why don't you just give me the book now. Okay?"

Ricky slapped the teacher's open palm in a low five. Flipping his own hand palm-up, he said, "Put 'er there, man!" Then he threw the diary back to Guillermo, who by now was standing on a desk of his own.

Becca shot a look at Mrs. Robeson to see how she would deal with this blatant disrespect, but a cheer from the boys directed her attention back to the kids. Guillermo sprung up from the desktop to hit a panel in the suspended ceiling. The panel, pushed off the grid, left a gap in the ceiling above Guillermo's head.

Gina reminds me of Kassy, she thought, recalling how her younger sister always managed to look fashionable and well-groomed. *Gina's clothes aren't exactly the latest fashion, but she carries herself like Kassy, too—with a kind of sassy and don't-mess-with-me attitude.* Becca grinned. She didn't care much about fashion, but she liked a girl who could stick up for herself like Gina did.

She tapped Gina lightly on the shoulder to get her attention. "Hi. I'm Becca," she said with a smile. "I guess you're Gina, huh?"

The younger girl looked at Becca but didn't return the smile. "Yep."

"I haven't seen you around before. Are you new here?"

"We're just here for a little while," the girl shot back quickly.

"Those boys were sure a pain today, huh?" Becca said, thinking maybe Gina was being abrupt because she was still upset over the scene with Ricky and Guillermo. "I've got a big brother named Matt, and he used to pick on me all the time. Ricky reminded me of him today."

"Ricky's not my brother," Gina said angrily, speeding up until she was practically running down the stairs.

"I know he's not. I just meant . . ." Becca began.

"Just because we live in the same place doesn't make us family," Gina said. Finding that she couldn't go any faster on the stairs because of the students ahead of them, she whirled to face Becca, hands on her hips. "Ricky's nothing but a shelter kid. He ain't even got a father. Me and my mom, we're only here for a little while. *My* father's coming back for us, just as soon as he finds work."

She glared at Becca, and slowly Becca understood what Gina was telling her. *She and Ricky live in the same place—the shelter. The homeless shelter here at the Center. She's not at the Center just for the summer program. She and her mother are homeless.* With the realization, Becca felt a pang of regret that was almost physical, as if a fist had struck her chest and nearly knocked the wind out of her. She met Gina's angry glare, then dropped her eyes to look more closely at the girl's faded but carefully coordinated outfit.

I guess I only feel bad about Gina because she reminds me of Kassy, Becca thought. Shame washed over her. *I never really thought about the kids in the shelter being kids like my sister—or me. Like Gina I figured I'm different from "shelter kids." Maybe even like we're different species. I should feel compassion for every kid who ends up in a homeless shelter!*

"My father *is* coming back," Gina repeated, maybe thinking that Becca's silence meant she didn't believe Gina. "He didn't abandon us. He just had to leave for a while to find work." She looked defiantly at Becca, as if daring her to contradict her.

"Sometimes dads have to do that," Becca agreed, even though it had never crossed her mind that her own dad would ever have to do something so difficult. "Sometimes dads have to do hard things for their kids. My little brother Alvaro—his dad couldn't take care of him, so he let us adopt Alvaro."

Gina's eyes narrowed. "My dad's not letting anybody adopt me. We're still a family—my dad and me and my mom."

"Of course!" Becca said quickly. Inwardly she was thinking, *Why do I always say the first thing that comes into my head? Now I've gone and upset the poor kid.* Aloud, she continued, "Alvaro didn't have a mom like you do—his mom died, so that made things different. What I meant was, just because a dad can't be around, that doesn't mean he doesn't love his kid."

Gina's expression softened. "Yeah," she said. Her voice was suspiciously husky, and Becca thought her eyes were moist. Gina ducked her head and started down the stairs again, as if she were embarrassed about becoming emotional, so Becca changed the subject.

"That's a pretty cool diary. I like the fur."

Gina clutched the little book tightly. "It's mine, and that Ricky's a jerk if he thinks he can just take it!"

Becca was about to reprimand Gina for calling Ricky names, when suddenly she thought, *I wonder how many things of her very own Gina has?* Recalling the limited space in the homeless shelter, Becca knew that Gina probably didn't have much. She thought about her own room at home, strewn with sports equipment and CDs and photos of her family and friends. *If all I had was a diary, I guess I'd be pretty possessive of it too.* Gently, she reached out and stroked the furry diary with one finger, hoping to show Gina she admired her possession without looking as if she wanted to take it.

Gina held out the book to Becca. "You can hold it if you want," she said generously. "I don't mind if *you* do. Just don't try reading it like that jerk Ricky," she added. "A diary is private. Everybody knows that!"

"I used to try to keep a journal, but I was always forgetting to write in it," Becca admitted.

"So did you just quit writing?" Gina asked.

"Uh-uh." Becca shook her head. "I decided to use my journal to write letters to God instead. Do you talk to God?"

Gina looked skeptical. "Not really, I guess. I don't think He cares very much about what I have to say."

"Do you know Jesus? He cares about everything about you."

Gina squirmed. "They talk about Jesus a lot here at the Community Center. All the time, Jesus, Jesus, Jesus. He's like, God's best friend or something, right?"

Becca smiled, a smile that came from inside and lit up her eyes and her whole face. "Jesus is God's own Son, and He *is* God. And you know what? He's *my* best friend. Can I tell you about Him? He could be your best friend too."

Gina only shrugged, but she didn't say no, so Becca ran to the gym to tell Mr. York and André that Gina would be away from the class for a little while. Then she grabbed two beanbag chairs from the library, settled herself and Gina into a quiet corner, and told the homeless girl about the Savior who gave up the best home in the world and said good-bye to the best Father in the world, becoming homeless Himself out of love for Gina.

Gina was obviously moved, although she tried to recover her tough-girl image, blinking back the moisture in her eyes and wiping her nose on the back of her hand with a little snort that Becca suspected disguised a sob.

"Gina, if you want Jesus for your best friend, I can help you pray right now," Becca suggested quietly. Inside, she was praying urgently, *Please, Jesus! Open Gina's heart to You!*

Gina gave a final, loud sniff and tossed her hair back out of her face. *Just like Kassy,* Becca thought, as she continued to pray silently for Gina's decision.

Gina looked at Becca for a long moment. "No, thanks," she said at last. "I don't think I want to pray right now."

Becca bit her lip in disappointment, then quickly tried to replace the expression of regret with a smile. *I don't want her to make the decision to please* me, she reminded herself. *I want her to make it because of Jesus.* "That's okay," she said. "Do you have any questions about Jesus?"

"Not really," Gina said, standing up and picking up the beanbag chair. She swung it, and the foam pellets inside made a rustling sound like wind blowing through leaves. "We better put these back and get to the gym, huh?"

Becca pulled herself to her feet and picked up her beanbag. Apparently Gina had heard all she was ready to hear—for now at least.

● ● ●

Becca spent the rest of the day working with André in the rec program. In the morning, classes rotated through the gym for structured fitness workouts and games, but in the afternoon the older kids had a large block of free recreation time. As usual, the middle-school boys needed the most attention to keep them from getting out of hand, so Becca spent most of the afternoon shooting hoops with Ricky and Guillermo and their buddies. At the end of one particularly sweaty game, after they'd all helped themselves to water from the five-gallon jugs André had out for them, Becca wandered over to the doorway where Ricky had plopped himself down to catch the breeze.

"How's it going, dude?" she asked, settling down next to him with her back against the wall. She didn't have to ask directly about Ricky's confrontation with Mrs. Robeson in her office; she knew Ricky well enough to know he'd tell her about it if he wanted to.

"It's cool," Ricky said. "Me and Guillermo have to do grounds work for a week—pick up trash in the parking lot and help the janitor sweep up at night—to pay for getting the ceiling fixed, but Mrs. R. ain't kicking us out or nothing."

Becca nodded. She knew it would take a lot more than roughhousing to get a kid kicked out of the Community Center programs—especially a kid like Ricky, who didn't have anywhere else to go. She didn't tell Ricky that, though; no point in letting him think he could get away with too much.

"She gave us a warning, though," Ricky added after a pause. "I ain't supposed to mess with that no-good Gina no more."

Becca stuck her legs out straight in front of her and examined her shoes. Without making eye contact with Ricky, she said casually, "I talked with Gina a little this morning. I don't think she's no good."

"Yeah, well, you don't have to see her 24/7," Ricky said. "I wish she'd never of come here. If it wasn't for her, I wouldn't have to move." His voice trembled, and Becca looked at him in surprise.

"Move? What do you mean?"

"I gotta move to the men's side in the shelter," Ricky said. He picked at a loose thread on the sideseam of his baggy shorts. "See, I've been sleeping on the women and kids' side with my mom and my little brother. It didn't matter to nobody because there wasn't any other older kids. But now Gina's here and somebody got to looking at the rules and they say I gotta sleep on the men's side 'cause I'm almost 13."

"I guess that makes sense." Becca could see that it wouldn't be appropriate for Gina and Ricky to share sleeping quarters. "It bothers you, though?"

Ricky stopped picking at the thread and looked Becca. She was surprised to see the tension in his face. "Becca, you ever been here at night?"

"No," Becca admitted.

"Well, some of those guys, they . . . well, they crazy! Not all of 'em, but some. Some of 'em get up and walk around at night and talk to themselves—just crazy! I didn't mind so much when I was just hearing them through the divider, but . . ." His voice trailed off.

Becca didn't know what to say. Her mom had explained to her that hospitals couldn't afford to keep mentally ill patients if they were well enough not to be a danger to themselves or others. But being well enough to leave the hospital didn't always mean being well enough to hold a job and afford an apartment, so a high percentage of mentally ill people—especially if they didn't have family looking out for them— ended up on the streets or in the shelters.

"That sounds kind of scary," Becca said.

Ricky just nodded.

"When do you move to the men's side?"

"Tonight."

"No wonder you were picking on Gina today," Becca said, voicing her thoughts without thinking about it. "I guess it seems like it's her fault."

"It *is* her fault!" Ricky said. "She's goes around thinking she's so important, and talking about how she's only gonna be here for a little while. I wish she'd just leave now!"

"I guess she wishes she could too," Becca said gently. "She's not so different from you that way, you know."

"Yeah, except I'm never getting out of here."

Becca looked at Ricky in surprise. "Why do you say that? Of course you'll move out of the shelter sometime."

"Nah." Ricky shook his head obstinately. "I got no place to go."

"Sure you do! Maybe not right away, but later on, once you're out of high school, you'll go to college . . ." Becca trailed to a stop at the defeated look on Ricky's face.

"Becca, ain't hardly nobody from the shelter graduates high school," Ricky said. "And *nobody* goes to college."

"You can, Ricky!" Becca said. "You don't have to drop out—you can do whatever you put your mind to—I know it!"

Ricky just shook his head. "Yeah, right. First I gotta survive sleeping with the crazies, though, don't I?"

chapter 3

"Hey, Matt! Did you know your boxers are pink?" Becca waved the offending underwear like a flag as she marched into her older brother's room, Saturday morning's basket of laundry balanced on one hip.

"Becca, I'm gonna get you for this!" Matt lunged for the boxers. Grabbing them and wadding them into a ball, he pelted Becca. "How am I going to explain this to the guys in the dorm?"

"Hey, it's not my fault," Becca said. "It's Kassy's turn to do the laundry this week. Go throw your underwear at her, not me!" She dumped the laundry basket on the bed, and Matt groaned as Becca's red practice jersey tumbled out along with more formerly white underwear. Becca picked up another pair of pink-tinted boxers. She held them up, looking from the boxers to Matt appraisingly. "I think it's your color," she said with a mischievous grin.

Matt made a face and headed out of his basement bedroom toward the laundry room. "I'd better check on what Kassy's doing with the next load," he told Becca over his shoulder, "before she shrinks my jock straps or something."

Becca rummaged through the clean laundry on Matt's bed to reclaim her jersey and anything else that might belong to her, but before she'd gotten to the bottom of the pile she heard Matt bellowing from the direction of the laundry room.

"KASSY!" he hollered. "There's water everywhere!"

Becca bolted for the door, her jersey tucked under one arm. She stopped short at the sight of sudsy water streaming across the floor. Matt plunged a hand into the overflowing laundry tub and pulled out a plastic bag. The water in the tub began to drain properly, but a steady stream still flowed across the concrete of the unfinished part of the basement toward Matt's bedroom door.

"Quick, Becca!" Matt said. "Mop it up before it gets to my carpet!"

Without thinking, Becca wadded her jersey into a long roll and put it on the floor just ahead of the sudsy stream. The jersey acted like a dam to redirect the water away from Matt's room, but it didn't soak up enough to stop the flow. So Becca dashed back into the bedroom, gathered up an armload of laundry from the bed, and started sopping up puddles wherever they formed. In less than a minute, she had the water mostly mopped up, and she sat back on her heels in satisfaction.

"Becca?" She heard Matt's quiet voice above her and looked up. He had a pained expression on his face. "Is that my *clean* laundry?"

Becca looked at the wads of sodden clothes around her and began to suspect that her quick action hadn't been quite as clever as it seemed at the time. She gave Matt a sheepish smile and shrugged.

"My clean laundry that I was going to pack before leaving for college tomorrow?" Matt persisted.

"Oops," Becca said. Cautiously she picked up a pink tube sock and squeezed it. A little shower of soapy water fell and formed a moat around the sock's mate. *Definitely not a clever move*, she decided. But as she looked at the soggy piles of pink underwear, she couldn't quite suppress a giggle. Then a chortle. Then a full-fledged belly-buster of a laugh. Before she knew it, Matt had tackled her and was pummeling her with soggy shorts, laughing as hard as she was.

"Gotcha pinned!" he said triumphantly as he hooked Becca's arms behind her back. But Becca thrust her legs into the air and used the leverage to roll over on top of him.

"Not likely, Joe Boxer," she retorted. Her agility was no match for Matt's six-foot bulk though, and before she knew it she was flat on her back again.

"Eat my shorts!" Matt grinned as he brandished a pair of boxers in Becca's face.

Before Becca could think of a snappy comeback, footsteps on the stairs attracted her attention.

"What in the world?" Mrs. McKinnon stood on the bottom step, hands on her hips, looking in astonishment at the laundry-strewn basement and her two oldest children wrestling in the middle of it. "What happened here?"

Matt stood up, wiping his damp hands on his pants. "The laundry tub overflowed," he explained. "I think Kassy left a plastic bag in it, and it plugged the drain."

"Did all the laundry overflow with it?" Mrs. McKinnon asked, raising her eyebrows.

"No, that was some creative engineering on Becca's part." Matt grinned at his sister and reached out a hand to pull her up off the floor. "I think she and Kassy are going to miss me so much that they've formed a conspiracy to keep me from going back to school." In response to his mother's questioning look, he explained, "That *was* clean laundry."

"Pink!" a little voice piped from behind Mrs. McKinnon. "Pink! Pink! The Cat in the Hat is back!" Alvaro pushed past Mrs. McKinnon, pointing gleefully at the pink piles.

"Huh?" Matt crouched down so his face was on a level with Alvaro's. "It's pink all right, but what's this about the Cat in the Hat, little bro?"

"The Cat in the Hat is back," Alvaro repeated with authority. "A-B-C-D . . ."

"It's the book Alvaro and I read together every night," Becca explained. "*The Cat in the Hat Comes Back*. You know—Dr. Seuss. The Cat in the Hat turns all the snow pink, and little cats from A to Z have to try to get it white again." She shrugged at Matt's blank expression.

"Do you think those little cats have an exclusive contract, or would they come and get my boxers white again?" Matt asked. He turned to Mrs. McKinnon. "Mom, I'm not sure Kassy is responsible enough to handle the family laundry."

"I'm a teenager now, just like you and Becca—and I'm perfectly responsible!" Kassy stomped down the basement stairs with more noise than seemed reasonable for her size. She glared at the soggy bag that Matt held toward her. "What?"

"If you were responsible, the machine wouldn't have overflowed because of *this*."

She put her hands on her hips in an unconscious imitation of her mother that made Becca and Matt exchange amused glances. "It wasn't *me* that put that bag in the tub."

"And it wasn't you who removed it, either," Matt pointed out.

"Why should I?" Kassy tossed her dark, shoulder-length hair and heaved a martyred sigh.

"Because you were the one doing the laundry?" Matt suggested patiently. "Because if the laundry tub is plugged, it overflows when the washer drains into it? Because my bedroom is in the basement and I don't like to have to swim to get to it? Do you find any of these reasons convincing?"

"I didn't put the bag there, so I don't see why it should be my job to take it out," Kassy insisted.

Matt took a deep breath, but Mrs. McKinnon interrupted. "The bag is out, so that's over. Thank you, Matt, for taking care of it. Becca and Kassy, you can clean up the rest of this mess."

"*I* didn't make this mess," Kassy began, but her mother quelled her with a look that all the kids knew meant the discussion was over.

"You'll just have time to throw them in the washer and start a new load before we leave for our hike. We want to have enough time for Alvaro's first rock climb," Mrs. McKinnon said, taking Alvaro's hand and heading up the stairs. "Oh, and Kassy—" she stopped and looked down at the laundry, her lips twitching ever so slightly, "put some bleach in it."

"Hear, hear!" Matt said. "You can run these through again too," he added, dumping the few remaining dry clothes from his bed into the laundry basket and carrying it out to Kassy. "Oh, wait!" He grabbed a pair of boxers and turned back to his room. "I'll need these. I want to change before we go hiking." He looked at the damp spots on his clothes. "I feel like a dog that's rolled in something nasty."

"There was a farmer had a dog, and Pinko was his name-o," Becca sang softly, winking at Kassy. She took one end of the laundry basket and Kassy took the other. Marching to the laundry room, they sang lustily in unison, "P-I-N-K-O, P-I-N-K-O . . ."

"Sisters!" Matt exclaimed, shutting his bedroom door.

● ● ●

"Here we are," Mr. McKinnon said as if no one could tell they'd reached the gravel parking strip at the trailhead. "Bear Lake trail."

The family piled out. Matt opened the tailgate and handed a backpack each to Kassy and Becca before strapping one on himself. Mr. McKinnon, who didn't like to drive in hiking boots, was changing out of his regular shoes, and Mrs. McKinnon was retying Alvaro's bootlaces. Straightening up from her task, she began what Becca always thought of as the "supply roll call."

"Lunch pack?" she called out.

"Check!" said Becca, peering at the sandwiches, apples, and granola bars in the backpack Matt had handed her.

"Rain gear?"

"Check!" Kassy sang out.

"Climbing gear?"

"Check!" said Matt.

"Water bottles?"

"Check!" the family replied in unison. Alvaro carefully unscrewed the cap on his canteen and took a swallow—made thirsty by the power of suggestion, Becca suspected.

"Sunscreen on?"

"Check!" they said again.

"I smeared some on Alvaro on the way here," Becca added.

"Good," said her mom. "He'll be well-protected then, because I put some on him at home before we left." She ruffled Alvaro's short, spiky black hair affectionately, but Becca saw her gaze linger on the scars on Alvaro's left arm. Over a year after Alvaro's burns, his skin grafts looked fully healed, but Becca knew that skin was still extra-tender and susceptible to sunburn. She caught her mother's eye and they exchanged smiles.

"Let's go, then," Mr. McKinnon said, locking the red Suburban. "We want to get to the lake before it gets too hot."

Kassy rushed to be first on the trail, and Mrs. McKinnon and Alvaro followed.

"Wait a second, Dad," Matt said quietly, putting his hand on his dad's arm to stop him. "Can you unlock the Suburban again? I've got something else I want to get out."

"What is it?" Becca asked curiously as Matt reached under an old blanket in the back.

"A surprise I made for Alvaro," Matt said, showing her. "Think he'll like it?"

"It's perfect!" Becca told him. "When are you going to give it to him?"

"As soon as he starts complaining that the hike is too long," Matt answered. "Which, according to my calculations, ought to be in about three minutes!"

Laughing in agreement, Becca and Mr. McKinnon followed Matt as he hurried to catch up with the others. Becca watched as Matt's long, strong legs brought him to Alvaro, whose bony little legs had to take nearly two steps for every one that Kassy was taking ahead of him. Matt slowed his stride to keep pace with the little boy.

Sure enough, it was only a couple of minutes before Alvaro started whining. "My legs hurt. Can I have a piggyback ride?" He turned a pleading look toward Matt, but his eyes widened and a smile creased his skinny face when he saw the hiking stick Matt held out to him.

"Is it mine, Brother Matt?" he breathed, taking the stick and running his hand over the smooth knob at the end. "Is it?"

Becca smiled at the nickname. When the McKinnons adopted Alvaro from Guatemala, Matt was away for his first year at college. So Mrs. McKinnon showed Matt's high school graduation picture to Alvaro regularly, telling him, "This is your brother Matt." Alvaro's English wasn't very good, but he got the connection—and the name. "Brother Matt" it was from then on. Becca teased Matt that he ought to become a monk to live up to the name.

"Yeah, it's yours, little bro," Matt told Alvaro. "Did you see this, too? It's a bear bell—it's to scare the bears away."

Alvaro shook the stick gingerly, and the sleigh bell hanging just below the top knob jingled cheerily. Encouraged, Alvaro grabbed the stick with both hands and lunged with mock ferocity at an imaginary bear, then strode confidently up the trail, tired legs apparently forgotten. Matt winked at Becca and she grinned back.

"Nice going," she whispered. "Maybe you should major in child psychology instead of earth sciences."

"The bear bell is a nice touch," Mr. McKinnon announced. "I don't know how much good it does for bears, but it will help us keep track of Alvaro. The black bears aren't such a problem," he went on. "It's the grizzlies you have to be worried about."

"Dad, there aren't any grizzlies in Colorado," Matt said.

"The best thing to do is to watch the droppings," Mr. McKinnon continued, as if he hadn't heard Matt. He had Kassy's and Mrs.

McKinnon's attention now too. "If it's a black bear dropping, it will be smooth and dark. If it's a grizzly, it will be lighter and lumpy—and have bells in it."

"Da-ad!" Becca and Kassy groaned. But Mrs. McKinnon laughed, and after a moment Alvaro joined in, even though Becca was pretty sure he didn't get the joke.

The mid-August sun blazed hot on Becca's back. She appreciated the parts of the trail that passed under the shady ponderosa pines or the flickering aspen leaves that made the sunlight seem to move like water on the trail. Every so often Mrs. McKinnon called a "hydration break," and the family would stop in the shade to drink from their canteens and water bottles. For Alvaro's sake, they set a slow and steady pace, so Becca didn't feel particularly tired, but she knew that even easy hiking in the mountains could lead to dehydration quickly because of the altitude.

At the end of one break, Alvaro pulled Becca's arm and held her back as the rest of the family started up the trail.

"Shh!" he whispered insistently. "Pat!"

"Pat?" Becca echoed blankly.

"Pat!" Alvaro repeated joyously, his eyes alight. Tugging Becca's arm, he crouched and pointed into the shadowy scrub along the trail. There sat a small rabbit, munching contentedly and apparently completely unconcerned about the two humans only three feet away. "Pat the bunny!" Alvaro said.

Becca grinned as she caught on. *Pat the Bunny* was one of Alvaro's favorite bedtime books before he graduated to *The Cat in the Hat*. It was really intended for even younger children, but because Alvaro was still learning English at the time, the story was just right for him. Each page of the book had a simple phrase and an action the child could do. The title of Alvaro's favorite page was "Pat the bunny," and he loved stroking the soft, furry rabbit in the book. Even though Becca tried to explain that he was *patting* the bunny, he remained convinced that the bunny was *named* Pat. Sort of like "Brother Matt," Becca supposed.

Now Alvaro was wriggling with delight at having discovered Pat, the bunny, in the very flesh. Quietly the two crouched and watched the bunny, who in turn watched them.

"He must be a very young bunny," Becca whispered. "He's so small."

"Uh-huh," Alvaro agreed, never taking his eyes off "Pat."

"Watch how his ears twitch." Becca picked up a small stone and dropped it on the rocky trail an arm's length away. The rabbit's ears swiveled at the sound.

"Good Pat," Alvaro soothed. "Good Pat."

"Do you see his funny nose?" Becca said. Alvaro wrinkled his own nose in imitation as the rabbit chewed.

At last Alvaro couldn't resist any longer, and he reached out a tentative hand. The rabbit tensed, and Becca held her breath, hoping it would stay long enough for the little boy at least to feel its fur. But as calm as the rabbit seemed, it was still a wild creature, and, while Alvaro's hand was still at least a foot away, "Pat" whirled suddenly and disappeared into the brush in a rustle of leaves.

"Oh . . . good-bye, Pat," Alvaro said. Becca was afraid he'd be heartbroken, but he turned a glowing face to her and said exultantly, "We saw Pat the bunny, Becca! We saw Pat the bunny!"

"We did, Alvaro, and *you* found him," Becca said, scooping Alvaro up in a hug then setting him back on his feet. "Let's go tell Mom, shall we?"

"Mama, Mama," Alvaro called, hurrying up the trail after the rest of the family. "We saw Pat! I almost toucheded him!"

Becca picked up Alvaro's hiking stick, which he'd left behind in his excitement, and followed. Alvaro's enthusiasm seemed to infect the rest of the family. Matt launched into a baritone rendition of "Little Bunny Foufou" and Kassy dropped her maturity pose and acted out all the motions.

"Your turn for a solo, Becca," Matt said when Little Bunny Foufou had exhausted his chances for good behavior and been turned into a goon. "Something with a good beat that we can hike to."

Becca thought a moment, then said, "This one's for you, Alvaro." She handed the hiking stick to him. "You can shake your bell to help me keep time." Clearing her throat importantly, she began:

The bear went over the mountain,
    the bear went over the mountain,
the bear went over the mountain,
    and what do you think he saw?

He saw some McKinnons hiking,
    he saw some McKinnons hiking,
he saw some McKinnons hiking,
    and what do you think he did?

He ate up all the McKinnons,
    he ate up all the McKinnons,
he ate up all the McKinnons,
    and what do you think they did?

She glanced at Alvaro, whose eyes were wide. With an encouraging nod and a smile, she went on:

They gave him a tummy ache,
    they gave him a tummy ache,
they gave him a tummy ache,
    and what do you think he did?

He burped up all the McKinnons,
    he burped up all the McKinnons,
he burped up all the McKinnons,
    and what do you think he did?

Becca had to stop a moment before the final verse, because Matt had punctuated the burping stanza with increasingly voluminous belches, and she needed to regain her composure before she could sing. Kassy and Alvaro were laughing so hard that they wouldn't have heard her if she'd gone on immediately anyway. When Alvaro clapped his hands and begged, "What did the bear do, Becca? What did the bear do?" she continued:

He never went over the mountain,
    he never went over the mountain,
he never went over the mountain
      to see what he could see.

"*Adios*, Bear!" Alvaro called, waving his hiking stick and jingling the bell.

"And hello, Bear Lake," Mr. McKinnon said from ahead on the trail. "We're here."

chapter 4

"Are you excited about your first climb, little bro?" Matt asked as he double-checked that Alvaro's climbing harness was secure and fastened the helmet strap under the little boy's chin.

"Maybe," Alvaro said hesitantly. The family had gone rock climbing a few times over the summer, and Alvaro had always decided just to watch. He had agreed to give it a try today because it was Matt's last weekend home before he went back to college for a pre-semester service project.

"You'll do great!" Becca assured him. "Matt's got your rope—you know he'll take good care of you."

Alvaro nodded seriously, then put his hand to his stomach. "Little cars are bumping around in my tummy," he confessed.

"Let me see," Mr. McKinnon said, carefully working Alvaro's T-shirt loose from under the harness and pulling it up to Alvaro's chin. Crouching down, he scrutinized the little boy's belly, then pressed his mouth to Alvaro's skin and buzzed his lips noisily. "There," he announced, straightening up as Alvaro giggled. "That's given those cars extra energy so they can help you climb. Let's go do it!"

"Kassy!" Mrs. McKinnon called. "Come over and watch!" Kassy left the fallen tree where she had been practicing the vaults she'd learned at gymnastics camp and joined the family at the base of the rock face.

Becca and Matt had already put a belay rope in place, so all that was left was to hook the rope to Alvaro's harness.

"Remember the commands?" Matt asked.

"Climbing," Alvaro responded tentatively.

"Not quite," Matt said. "You forgot the very first one."

"Belay on?" Alvaro asked.

"On belay!" Matt said.

"On belay!" Alvaro shouted.

Matt smiled. "Belay on, my man."

"Climbing!"

"Climb on!" Matt answered enthusiastically.

Cautiously, Alvaro reached out for toeholds and handholds on the rock face and began inching his way up.

"You're doing it, Alvaro!" encouraged Mrs. McKinnon.

"You look just like Spiderman!" Becca said. "You're a superhero!"

Alvaro peeked over his shoulder to grin down at them, but quickly turned his head back as he felt his body shift out a little from the rock.

"You're okay!" Matt assured him, taking up the slack on the belay rope. "Trust the rope, Alvaro. You won't fall."

Mrs. McKinnon snapped pictures on the digital camera as Alvaro worked his way up the rock face. As his confidence grew, he moved more quickly, but about two-thirds of the way up, the climb—while still a beginner's route—got a little more difficult. The holds were farther apart and, for a first-timer, harder to find. Alvaro slowed down again and began to murmur fretfully.

"It's too hard," he called down.

"You're doing great," Matt called back. "Keep going—you're almost there."

"But my arms hurt," Alvaro whined.

"Let your legs do the work. Push up with your legs instead of pulling so much with your arms," Matt suggested.

"My legs hurt too."

"Be tough, Spiderman," Becca told him. "You can do it!"

Alvaro persisted for a few more feet, then got stuck. He clung to the rock, groping for handholds but not finding anything big enough to get a grip on.

"I can't do it!" he wailed.

"Sure, you can!" Mr. McKinnon encouraged.

"There's a good handhold a little to your right," Matt called up to Alvaro. "No, a little farther . . . Keep reaching . . ."

"I can't do it!" Alvaro cried again. "I'm scared!"

"Let me go up and help him," Becca said to Matt. As Matt nodded, she moved to the rock face.

"Becca, is that safe?" asked her dad. "Shouldn't you be roped in?"

"Nah—this beginner route is practically a scramble," Becca assured him. "I'll be fine."

"Really, she will, Dad," Matt said. "Becca's an experienced climber. She knows what she can do and what she can't."

"I've never seen that stop her from trying," murmured Mrs. McKinnon, but she gave Becca a nod, and Becca swarmed easily up the rock toward Alvaro.

"Hey, big guy," she said as she reached his side. "Now there's two of us up here. How's that?"

Alvaro smiled weakly, his face a little paler than its usual coppery tan. "Good," he said.

"See where my hand is?" Becca asked, reaching over to grip a small ledge above Alvaro's head. "Can you reach that?"

Nodding slightly, Alvaro stretched to rest his fingers on the ledge. Becca saw a little of the tension leave his body.

"Great! Now look down just a little—not all the way down; just to my foot. See that ledge? That's a perfect place for your foot."

Cautiously Alvaro put the toe of his boot into the foothold Becca indicated. He exhaled loudly and relaxed a little more. Bit by bit, Becca coaxed him up to the top of the rope, pointing out holds when Alvaro couldn't find them, praising him lavishly every time he made progress.

"Hey, Alvaro," she said at last. "Look up."

Alvaro took his eyes off his last handhold and raised his head. He gave a relieved laugh that came out half like a snort when he saw the carabiner at the end of the climb just above his head.

"You made it to the top, man," Becca said. "Reach up and touch the carabiner."

Alvaro did, and gave Becca a huge grin.

"Alvaro!" Mrs. McKinnon called from below. "Smile for the camera!"

Clutching the rope, Alvaro twisted his upper body to pose for a victory shot. Looking down for the camera, his smile froze and Becca saw his body stiffen.

"Oooh," he breathed. "A long way down."

Uh-oh, Becca thought. *I'd better get him moving before he has time to really freak out.* Aloud, she said, "Remember the commands for rappelling down?"

"On belay," Alvaro quavered, too softly for anyone but Becca to hear. She relayed it down to Matt.

"Belay on," Matt called back.

"Okay, Alvaro," Becca said in her calmest voice. "You can stop looking down now. Hold tight to the rope and look at your hands."

Alvaro seemed frozen for a long moment, then with a visible effort turned his head and clutched the rope so tightly that Becca could see his knuckles turning white.

"You're all set," Becca said. "Now just lean back and walk down the rock."

"I *am* leaning back," Alvaro said, his body pressed snugly against the rock.

"Hmm. Well, lean back just a little farther, okay?" Becca grasped

Alvaro's rope and pushed her upper body away from the rock to demonstrate.

Alvaro leaned an inch or two away from the rock and gasped. "I'm falling!"

"No, you're not. You're tied into your harness and your harness is attached to the rope. And Matt has the other end of the rope. He won't let you fall." Becca gave her little brother an encouraging smile. "Listen, forget about leaning back. Just sit in your harness. Pretend it's a chair, okay?"

Cautiously, Alvaro shifted his weight from his feet to his little rear end. When he realized he could rest on the harness without falling, he let out a sigh, and Becca realized he'd been holding his breath.

"Atta boy, Alvaro!" Matt called up. "Trust the rope."

"Now just pretend you're Spiderman and walk down the rock," Becca told him. "I'll be right beside you."

Alvaro lifted a foot off the ledge and took one unsteady step down the rock, then another.

"Becca!" he cried. "I'm doing it!"

"You sure are," Becca said. "Race you to the bottom!"

As Becca had hoped, Alvaro's natural love for speed overcame the last of his fear, and he leaned back from the rope so he could move his feet faster. Matt let him down at a safe and steady pace, and Becca made sure to climb down just a little more slowly than Alvaro's descent.

Alvaro reached the ground a few seconds before Becca and jumped on her, harness and all, as soon as she touched the ground.

"We did it, Becca! We did it!"

Becca gave him a hard squeeze, then set him on the ground, holding on to steady his limbs, which were trembling with a mixture of adrenaline and fear that she remembered from her own first climb. Matt and Kassy high-fived Alvaro while Mrs. McKinnon clicked away on the camera.

"Well done," Mr. McKinnon told Alvaro. "What did you think of your first climb?"

Alvaro wriggled all over with pride and excitement. "Can I do it again?"

• • •

Kassy took a turn climbing, and then Alvaro climbed again, and by that time everyone was hungry for the sandwiches and fruit Mrs. McKinnon had packed. Kassy and Alvaro took off their climbing shoes and ate their lunch while splashing ankle-deep in the icy mountain lake. Mr. and Mrs. McKinnon found a relatively flat rock nearby, where Mrs. McKinnon alternated eating with snapping shots of the kids and the scenery. Matt grabbed a couple of sandwiches and pointed to a big, flat rock about 30 feet farther along the shoreline.

"Come on, Bec. Let's eat over there."

Becca picked out a peanut-butter-on-tortilla sandwich, crammed an apple in the cargo pocket of her shorts, and followed Matt as he picked his way among the boulders tumbled along Bear Lake.

"Still no bears," Becca teased as they settled themselves on the sun-warmed rock jutting out over the lake.

"Nope." Matt spoke through a mouthful of bologna and mustard.

Becca squinted at the snow fields on the mountains rising high above the lake. "Are those part of the glaciers, do you think?"

Matt shielded his eyes and studied the snow a while. "I think maybe that greenish part to the right—no, *that* right—" he said, pulling Becca by the nose so that she was looking right instead of left. "That might be year-round ice, which would make it technically glacier. The rest of it I'm pretty sure is just winter snow that will be gone by the end of summer."

"This *is* the end of summer," Becca reminded. "At least, it's the end of summer vacation. It'll seem weird to have you gone again."

"It was kind of weird to come home, actually," Matt admitted. "I wasn't sure what it would be like to come home to a new brother—and to Mom and Dad's rules after being on my own for a school year."

"How was it?"

"Different," Matt said. "Different, but good. Alvaro's a great little bro, and Mom and Dad—well, you have to admit it: They're pretty terrific parents."

"You know, you're different too," Becca said.

"Yeah?" Matt turned from studying the view to study Becca. "How's that?"

"Well, for one thing, you used to be such a basketball freak," Becca said. "Why did you give up your spot on the team? I still don't get that. You always dreamed of playing b-ball for college. Why would you do something like that?"

Matt stared out at the lake for a while, as if thinking how best to explain. "It's kind of a long story," he said at last.

"I've got time."

"We had this chapel speaker toward the beginning of the year," Matt said, a faraway look coming into his eyes. "He challenged us to pick a 'life verse'—a verse we could use to guide our decisions and shape our direction. I chose Philippians 3:14: 'I press on toward the goal to win the prize for which God has called me heavenward in Christ Jesus.'"

Matt fell silent, and Becca waited a while, thinking this wasn't such a very long story if Matt wasn't going to say any more. Finally she said, "Okay, I'm dense. How was that a message from God to quit basketball? It sounds more like a challenge to keep going."

"Uh-huh." Matt nodded. "But the thing is, the goal I was pressing toward changed. Basketball wasn't it anymore." He leaned back on his elbows and looked at Becca. "Do you remember the stone sign right in front of campus?"

Becca nodded. She'd seen it when the family went to visit Matt for Parents' Weekend last fall. "'For Christ and His kingdom,'" she quoted.

"That's the college mission statement, and I decided to make it mine, too," Matt said. "So I started volunteering in the community, and I discovered you don't have to go on a missions trip to do missions. There's work to do for Christ and His kingdom right where you live."

Becca nodded. "Like at Outreach Community Center."

"Exactly. There's a community center a lot like Outreach not too far from campus," Matt said. "I got involved in tutoring in their after-school program, and pretty soon I was hooked." He pointed to Kassy and Alvaro, who had left the water and were poking around the minuscule strip of beach between the boulders, picking up stones and skipping them—or in Alvaro's case, trying to skip them. "Kids Kassy's and Alvaro's age have never gotten out of the city there. Some of them have never skipped stones in a lake or even been to a beach. None of them get a chance to face down their fears and find out what they can do the way Alvaro did today on that rock climb."

Together they watched as Kassy picked up a stone, gave it to Alvaro, then helped him skim it over the water. Alvaro jumped and cheered when the stone skipped twice instead of sinking immediately.

"I almost never see stuff like that," Matt said. "Kids working together, helping each other out. Most of the kids have never learned to work together. About the only way they know how to relate is to compete or to fight."

Becca thought about Ricky and Gina. She had to admit that Matt's description of the kids he worked with was a pretty good description of them and some of the other kids at Outreach Community Center, too. "Are there any kids at Outreach who have never been hiking in the mountains?" she wondered aloud.

"Ask," Matt suggested. "I bet there are lots."

"Really?" Becca found it hard to believe. "I mean, we're talking about the town of Copper Ridge. We're right *in* the mountains."

"Sure," Matt agreed. "But how many of the kids at Outreach have parents with cars reliable enough to get out of town and take the steep mountain roads? How many have parents with the time or money to take them out for a day? Aren't most of the parents either looking for work or working low-paying jobs with long hours?"

Becca nodded. "I guess I never thought about what kids do when they're not at the Center," she admitted. "I always figured being there was good enough. But I guess for some of the kids—the ones who sleep at the shelter—that's all they have."

"It's *great* for kids to be at the Center," Matt assured her. "And at the community center near my college, too. Shoot, I think it's so important, I gave up the basketball team so I could have enough time to volunteer there."

"Is that why you're not dating anybody, either?"

"Partly," Matt agreed. "My college courses are pretty demanding, and I've been trying to focus on the things that are most important. I just don't have the time and energy to balance everything I'm doing now *and* work on a relationship. At least not a serious one."

Becca opened her mouth to ask another question, but Matt asked her one first.

"So what about you and Nate?" he asked. "How serious is that?"

"Oh, I don't know," Becca said, smiling and clasping her arms over her chest in a gesture that was half a shrug and half hugging to herself the warm, bubbles-fizzing-inside feeling she got whenever she thought about Nate Visser. "I mean, we're not 'serious' like thinking about marriage. But we're not seeing anybody else, either."

"I'd figured that out for myself," Matt said dryly. "He's only over at the house every Friday night."

"With the rest of my friends," Becca pointed out. "We've always hung out at our house on weekends; you know that."

Matt nodded. "Seriously, though, Becca, I'm glad you haven't dumped your friends for Nate. I see too many people who spend all their time with a boyfriend or girlfriend and drop all their other friends."

"Dump the Brios?" Becca said, referring to her group of friends by the nickname they'd had since seventh grade. "Never! I can't see dropping Nate or basketball, either. Haven't you given up an awful lot just to tutor kids?"

Matt laughed. "Not *just* to tutor kids! That's looking at it the wrong way. I'm not just helping with homework—I'm changing kids' lives.

Once I saw those kids, how could I walk away just so I could play basketball? Shoot, Becca—I'm a McKinnon. Have you ever known anyone in our family who was satisfied to leave things the way they are without trying to make them better?"

Becca grinned. *Like Mom at Outreach Community Center,* she thought. *She's been battling the zoning board for months trying to expand the homeless shelter. And Dad at work. Didn't he just revamp the whole company's project management system?* She pressed her fist to her mouth and unconsciously gnawed the skin on her knuckle. *I'm the same way,* she thought. *I'm a make-it-better McKinnon too.* Staring unseeing across the lake, she thought about all the effort she and her friends had put into saving their friend Solana's family ranch from developers. *That was definitely making things better! And the Bible study group I started last spring—it kind of fizzled over the summer, but once school starts up, the Brios and I will get it going again. Jacie and Tyler and Solana and Hannah will help.*

Becca dropped her fist and smiled, thinking of all the things she'd dragged her friends into—the Bible study group, volunteering at the Center . . . *And sometimes some things I shouldn't have dragged them into,* she admitted to herself, remembering how she had dived into some less positive situations, taking Solana right along with her without thinking things through. *It's no wonder they tease me about being the "go for it" girl,* she thought.

She pulled her thoughts back to her conversation with Matt. "So—is it working? Are you making things better?"

Matt gave a suddenly boyish smile, like a little kid caught telling tall tales. "Not all by myself," he admitted. "But as part of the community program I am. If it hadn't been for wanting to spend the summer here so I could get to know Alvaro, I would have stayed at school over the summer and worked at this great camp for underprivileged kids. I might do that next year. I really want to make a difference for God. *That's* the goal I'm going for—not just tutoring or getting good grades or doing well in sports."

Becca's eyes lit up. "Making a difference for God—that's what I want to do! That's why I volunteer at Outreach Community Center." An exciting idea began unfolding in Becca's imagination. "Matt—what if we both made things better for kids at the centers—you at the community center near college and me at Outreach in Copper Ridge? Wouldn't that be awesome?"

Matt reached over to grasp Becca's hand, shaking it in the thumbs-over/thumbs-under "secret" handshake they used to use when they were kids. "Deal!" he said, spitting on their joined fists.

"Euew!" Becca pulled her hand free and wiped it on Matt's shirt. "Grow up! Is that what they teach you in college?"

"Expectoration 101. Required course," Matt said. "But seriously, Bec, think what it would be like if every Christian really made a difference for Christ and His kingdom. The world would never be the same!"

"The world never *will* be the same—at least not our little parts of it," Becca said with conviction.

"So what do you think you'll do to make Outreach Community Center better?" Matt asked. "Work on getting that zoning variance so they can enlarge the homeless shelter?"

"Nah—Mom's got that covered," Becca said. "I've got a different idea. I want to get kids like Ricky and Gina out here to hike and climb and camp." She told Matt about her conversation with Ricky earlier in the week. "He really doesn't think he can succeed," she concluded. "I think he'd change his mind if he could just accomplish something like rock climbing, though." She shot a sideways glance at her brother. "Think that sounds stupid?"

"Not a chance! Just look at Alvaro." Matt pointed to the little boy, who was busily scrambling up a boulder near the edge of the lake. When he got to the top he pounded his skinny little chest and let out a high-pitched approximation of what Becca could only assume was a Tarzan yell.

"Yeah, he thinks he's king of the mountain now, that's for sure," she laughed. "I bet I could help Ricky and Gina and the other kids feel like that too. I *know* I could!"

"With God's help," Matt reminded her.

"Exactly," said Becca. "Hey! That will be *my* life verse: *I can do all things through Christ who gives me strength.*" She said it again, and the words seemed so right that they were almost like candy in her mouth. "I'll have to find out where that is in the Bible."

"Philippians 4:13," Matt said.

"Wow! They really do teach you a lot at college," Becca teased.

"Dope." Matt rapped his knuckles on Becca's head. "I learned that in Sunday school. It's a good thing at least *one* of us paid attention."

"I can do all things . . ." Becca said it again. "I like it. What's your verse again, Matt?"

"I press on toward the goal to win the prize for which God has called me heavenward in Christ Jesus."

"And your goal is making a difference for God," Becca said.

Matt nodded. "It's a big goal. Do you see now why I gave up the basketball team? Because if I'm going to reach my goal, I've got to stay really focused. So to answer that question you asked a while back—no, I don't think I'm giving up a lot! I'm going after a lot more! Sometimes I get so excited just thinking about it that I can't sit still!"

Suddenly Matt leaped to his feet and began beating his chest and letting out his own ear-splitting Tarzan yells. "Ai-ee-ai-ee-ah!" he howled, jumping up and down on the rock. His heavy boots pounded a percussion beat that echoed off the steep rock walls.

Becca laughed until her sides hurt. This was the crazy brother Matt she knew from his high school days. It was good to know that the serious, mission-minded Matt still loved to have fun.

Now Matt had incorporated untying his hiking boots into his gyrations. Finally getting them loose, he kicked off the boots and pulled off his socks. With a final stupendous yell, he rushed to the edge of the rock and did a shallow dive into Bear Lake.

"Yow!" he yelled as he surfaced in the frigid water. "Refrrrreshing!"

Over on the "beach," Kassy and Alvaro applauded, and Mrs. McKinnon lifted the camera for a photo. Matt was already freestyling rapidly to the shore—Becca guessed that a quick dip was more than long enough at that temperature.

Becca gathered up the trash from her lunch and Matt's and began working her way among the boulders back to the rest of her family, carrying Matt's boots and socks with her. *What a perfect day for Matt's last weekend home*, she decided. *I'm glad we spent it together.* Suddenly she realized that the jealousy she had sometimes felt about Matt when they were both in high school was gone. *I was always trying to keep up with Matt*, she thought, *but now I look up to him. He's changed since he's been at college—in good ways.* Standing a little taller she thought, *Maybe I'm changing in good ways too. Making a difference for God! I can do all things through Him!*

She joined the rest of the family just as Matt was wading to shore. He shook himself like a dog, and Kassy and Alvaro leaped back, shrieking as droplets of cold mountain lake water sprayed them.

"Who wants a Bear Lake bear hug?" Matt bellowed, lumbering toward them with wet arms extended.

Kassy ran to Becca and yanked Becca in front of her like a shield. Watching Matt approach, Becca poked her elbow backward to nudge her sister. "Kassy—look." She gave a loud wolf whistle and Kassy giggled.

Matt stopped in mid-lumber. "What's so funny?" he demanded. "I'm supposed to be scaring the pants off you."

"More like the pants off *you*," Becca said, pointing to where Matt's shorts, heavy and dripping with lake water, sagged down to reveal a strip of his boxers.

"Nice underwear, Matt," Kassy said. "You look real pretty in pink."

chapter

DEAR GOD,

I CAN HARDLY BELIEVE MY SENIOR YEAR OF HIGH SCHOOL STARTS TODAY! I WANT TO MAKE IT OUTSTANDING! NOT JUST FOR ME, BUT FOR MY FRIENDS, AND MOST OF ALL FOR YOU. THERE'S SO MUCH I WANT TO DO—HELP OUR BASKETBALL TEAM WIN THE STATE CHAMPIONSHIP, DECIDE WHAT COLLEGE TO GO TO, FIND A WAY TO GET THE KIDS FROM THE COMMUNITY CENTER OUT ROCK CLIMBING. THERE'S SO MUCH I'M LOOKING FORWARD TO—GETTING THE BRIO BIBLE STUDY GOING AGAIN, GOING TO HOMECOMING AND PROM WITH NATE ☺, GRADUATION!!!!

Becca stopped writing in her journal to look at the picture of Nate pinned to her bulletin board. The seniors at Stony Brook High School had all had their pictures taken in the summer, and Becca had a wallet-sized copy of all five of Nate's poses. Her favorite was the most casual; Nate, wearing shorts and a polo shirt, sat on the studio floor in front of a plain white fabric drape. He was leaning sideways with one hand on the floor to support him and the other arm resting on his knee. The photographer had managed to capture a sense of the energy that Becca found so attractive in Nate, so that even though he was sitting, something about the way he was leaning slightly forward suggested that any second he would spring up and start moving.

Becca smiled at the familiar features in the photo—Nate's crisp, dark hair, short along the sides and a little longer at the top; his intense blue eyes under thick black eyebrows; the dimples that turned into generous laugh lines whenever he grinned. The loose-fitting polo shirt Nate wore in the picture didn't hide his broad shoulders and athletic build. *Of course, it's character that counts,* Becca murmured, echoing her mother's repeated refrain. *And Nate sure is a character!* She chuckled quietly, remembering how long it had taken Nate to get up the courage to ask her to Homecoming—their first date—last year. She had quickly learned that Nate was more than just a good-looking basketball player. Besides sharing her love of sports and fun, he was one of the first guys (besides her buddy Tyler, who was more like a brother than a "typical" guy) who had talked honestly about his thoughts and his questions about God.

Becca forced her gaze away from Nate's photos to the two pictures on either side of a cross that hung in the middle of her bulletin board. One picture was of her best friend, Solana Luz. Solana seemed to be thinking more about God lately than she ever had before, but she still had more questions than faith. With a hint of a frown creasing her forehead, Becca bent to her journal again.

not to be pushy, God, but please don't forget that this is solana's last year of high school too. she really needs to get

TO KNOW JESUS BEFORE SHE GOES AWAY TO
COLLEGE NEXT YEAR. I CAN'T BELIEVE I WANT
THAT FOR HER MORE THAN YOU DO, AND I
WANT IT A WHOLE LOT, SO I THINK YOU MUST
REALLY WANT IT A WHOLE LOT, AND YOU CAN
MAKE IT HAPPEN, SO—

Becca broke off and shook her head to clear the thoughts that were racing ahead of her writing. She reread her jumbled last sentence, then closed her eyes tight and took a deep breath to slow herself down.

OOPS. I GUESS I'M TRYING TO TELL YOU YOUR
BUSINESS AGAIN, GOD. I'M SORRY. I JUST GET
IMPATIENT, YOU KNOW? WELL, OF COURSE YOU
KNOW. ANYWAY, YOU TELL ME I CAN ASK YOU
FOR THE THINGS THAT ARE IMPORTANT TO ME,
AND SOLANA IS IMPORTANT. PLEASE LET HER
GET TO KNOW YOU SOON. AND PLEASE USE ME
IF THAT'S HOW YOU WANT TO DO IT.
AND THEN THERE'S OTIS.

Becca didn't have a picture of Otis, so she had put a photo cut from a paragliding magazine and the phone message about him on the other side of the cross on her bulletin board. Over the summer she'd gotten into a pattern of praying for Solana and Otis every time she wrote in her journal. She saw Solana practically every day, so she always had something about Solana to talk over with God. But she hadn't seen Otis since his paragliding accident and that was—she counted off the months since April—five months ago. Her prayers for Otis were getting pretty stale.

KEEP OTIS SAFE, LET HIM GET TO KNOW
JESUS, AND PLEASE LET HIM GET IN TOUCH
WITH ME SOMEHOW.

A car horn blared in the driveway, and Becca slammed her journal shut and crammed it into the already stuffed top drawer of her desk. "That's Jacie!" she yelled at no one, bounding down the stairs. "Tell her I'm coming!"

"When *I* have a boyfriend," Kassy commented, looking up from her breakfast cereal as Becca dashed into the kitchen, "I'll ride with *him* to school, not with a bunch of girls."

"That's because there's no other 'bunch of girls' like the Brios," Becca said. "We *always* start the school year together, and not even Nate is going to change that." She scooped her backpack up from the floor and ran out the side door to the metallic green Toyota Tercel idling in the driveway.

Jacie leaned out the driver's side window and blew kisses to Alvaro, who had followed Becca out into the driveway. Alvaro giggled and ducked his head shyly, then quickly looked up again to smile back at Jacie. *Everybody smiles at Jacie,* Becca thought. *It's not just the glossy dark curls, or her great coffee-with-cream complexion. It's something sunshiny from deep inside Jacie—something that lets you know right away that Jacie cares about you. Who else would drive all over town picking up friends so we could all go to school together?*

Becca pulled open the passenger's side door and leaned into the little two-door car. "Hey, hey, we're the Brios," she sang to the old Monkees theme song. "Great-est seniors around!"

Solana, in the front seat, grabbed an imaginary mike from the air and picked up the next line: "We're too busy . . . uh . . ."

"Senior-ing?" chimed in Jacie.

"Studying?" suggested Hannah from the backseat, with a teasing glint in her blue eyes.

"Flirting!" Solana declared, flipping her dark hair and giving her best sultry pout.

"Explaining that we're late for the first day of class because we had a gig in Becca's driveway?" Hannah said, looking at the gold watch clasped around her slender wrist.

"Party pooper!" Becca complained. "Get out, Sol, and let me in."

"Okay, but I've got shotgun."

Jacie rolled her eyes and murmured to Hannah, "Here we go again. Another argument about who gets the front seat."

"My legs are longer than yours," Becca pointed out to Solana. "You sit in the back."

"Hannah's legs are longer than yours, and she's okay in the back," Solana said.

"Yeah, but Hannah's nicer than I am." Becca said it with a grin, but she knew it was true.

"Got that right!" Solana said. "And you're nicer than I am, so get in the back."

"Chill!" Jacie cut in. She ran her fingers through her hair in an exasperated motion that set her spiral curls jiggling. "*I'll* sit in the back and one of you can drive."

Becca slid quickly into the backseat beside Hannah. "Jacie the peacemaker," she said. "Don't you know that we're just teasing?"

"I know that," Jacie said, putting the car in gear and backing out of the driveway. "What I don't know is why."

"'Cause we're so much alike," Becca said at the same moment that Solana said, "'Cause we're so different." They both laughed.

"Okay," said Becca as soon as Jacie turned onto the street and started toward school. "Senior year! What are we going to do to make it amazing? Let's make some plans."

"She does this every year," Solana told Hannah. "Tries to bully us into all kinds of projects. I don't know why we put up with her."

"'Cause you'd be bored silly without me," Becca said. "Lost in the lab, that's where Solana would be. Stuck in science. Hamstrung by horses." She tried to think of more alliterative phrases to describe Solana's interests, but Solana interrupted.

"Hamstrung by horses? What kind of sense does that make?"

"Exactly," Becca said, as if that proved her point. "No sense at all.

That's why we need to get organized. When shall we start up the Brio Bible study?"

Eagerly the girls discussed the group they had started toward the end of last school year. Meant as a place where anyone could ask honest questions about what the Bible says about God and about life, the group had attracted kids who believed the Bible is true as well as kids just checking it out. Becca, as the coordinator, was up front about her faith, but others, like Solana, were equally up front about not being ready to commit.

"I hope Kara comes again," Becca said. "You spent more time with her this summer than I did, Sol. Do you know if she's planning on it?"

Solana had invited Kara to the first meeting of the Brio Bible study and Kara had been to every meeting from then on till the group stopped meeting at the end of the school year.

"How should I know? She did keep asking *me* questions about God." Solana rolled her eyes. "As if—"

"Shoot." Becca was annoyed with herself. She had meant to follow up with Kara over the summer, but she just never got around to it. *Some leader I am*, she thought.

"If the Holy Spirit wants Kara there, she'll be there," Hannah said. Becca flashed her a grateful smile. Hannah used to drive her crazy with what Becca first thought was nothing but "church talk," but over the year they'd been friends Becca had learned that Hannah really meant what she said. She just said it in ways that sounded a little more spiritual than Becca was used to hearing high school students talk.

"Next you'll be telling me the Holy Spirit is what's getting *me* to the group," Solana said with a snort.

"Oh, no, Solana," Hannah said with a deceptive sweetness. "I wouldn't dream of telling you that. I'm waiting for you to figure it out on your own."

"Change of subject," Solana said. Becca caught Jacie's eye in the rearview mirror and sent her a knowing smile. Solana was ready to argue about anything she could keep at a safe intellectual distance; it was only when a subject starting hitting close to home that she backed off. Becca figured it was a good sign that Solana was feeling nervous that the Holy Spirit might be having an impact on her. She gave Hannah a thumbs-up that Solana couldn't see, then starting telling her friends about her ideas for taking Ricky, Gina, and the other kids from the Community Center out onto the mountain trails.

When they pulled into the Stony Brook High parking lot, Becca felt the familiar mix of feelings she had every new school year: part regret that the fun and freedom of summer was over, and part excitement in anticipation of seeing school friends and getting back into school sports. As for classes—well, she supposed she'd survive those. She had a couple of her favorite teachers for her demanding senior courses, and a couple of easier courses that should help her keep her GPA high enough to get her a reasonable chance of college scholarships.

But the best part of senior year at Stony Brook High was definitely the guy she saw leaning against the light pole in the parking lot, waiting for her to arrive. Nate Visser—all 6 feet 2 inches of him.

Nate hadn't noticed Jacie's Tercel yet, so Becca had a chance to study him without his knowing. He looked perfectly relaxed, as if he had the patience to wait as long as it took. But even his loose-limbed slouch had a hint of control rather than laziness about it, suggesting he could move into action at a moment's notice. With his long arms crossed across his chest, he looked confident—not in an arrogant kind of way, but as if he was ready to handle whatever might happen next. Just watching him made Becca go all carbonated inside, as if little Mountain Dew bubbles were fizzing through her.

"She's gone again," Solana said, waving her hand in front of Becca's face to interrupt her gaze. "Mooning over Mr. Tall, Dark, and Handsome."

"No, I'm not," Becca denied.

"She is," Jacie agreed. "You can tell by the dopey smile she gets."

Becca pulled her lips into a scowl, then gave it up and laughed. "I was just admiring the view," she said. "Admit it: He's not half bad."

"He's above average, I'll give you that," Solana said. "How come you're the least boy-crazy of us all and you get the steady boyfriend?"

"I am not boy-crazy!" Jacie and Hannah protested in unison.

"Ha!" Solana snorted. "You just don't admit it like I do." She pointed a finger at Hannah. "And don't give me any of that courtship talk. Just because you don't date doesn't mean you don't look."

Hannah's fair skin turned rosy under her tan, and the other girls looked at each other with raised eyebrows.

"She's blushing," Becca announced.

"Who is he, Hannah?" Jacie asked.

"Nobody," Hannah said, ducking her head so that her blonde hair swung like a silky curtain between her and her friends.

"There's definitely somebody," Solana stated. "It's written all over her."

"Maybe it's the guy who gave her gifts—"

"Out with it," Becca ordered. "Or we'll have to stalk you till we find out for ourselves."

"It's not like that," Hannah insisted. "It's just . . ."

"What?" demanded the three girls in unison as Hannah hesitated.

"Well," Hannah said, a smile dancing around the edges of her mouth, "last Thursday when I got off work, I went out to my car and there was a yellow rose under the windshield wiper."

"Oooh! Romantic!" Jacie said.

"Again?" Solana asked. "How do you do it, girl?"

"I don't know!"

"He must have left some sort of clue," Becca said.

Hannah shook her head. "There wasn't a note or anything."

"You must have some idea," Becca said. "Some guy who was flirting with you while you were hanging out in Copperchino or in the ice cream store or something."

Hannah shook her head. "Nobody like that came in that day."

"It must be your secret admirer again! You are *so* lucky!" Jacie said. "This is *so* unfair. Becca has Nate, Solana has Ramón—"

"Who is going to MIT in a few months," Solana interrupted. "After which I'll be just as lonesome as you are."

"—and Hannah has a secret admirer," Jacie continued, ignoring Solana. She pushed her lower lip into a pout. "What's the matter with me?"

"Too short," Solana said immediately.

"Too perky," Becca said.

"You two are terrible!" Hannah said. "Try a little encouragement for once!" Turning to Jacie, she said, "We love you exactly the way you are."

"Yeah," Becca agreed. "Short and perky."

"Who's short and perky?" Tyler Jennings stuck his head in through Jacie's window and pulled one of her corkscrew curls. "You must be talking about Jacie."

"I am not short and perky," Jacie said with dignity, pushing her door open so that Tyler had to scuttle backward to avoid decapitation. "I'm petite and . . . and . . . vivacious!"

"And a senior!" reminded Becca, kicking the back of Solana's seat to urge her out. She slid out of the car and waved wildly to attract Nate's attention. "Come on, guys! Let's get going! Stony Brook High will never be the same!"

chapter 6

Nate fell in step alongside Becca as the friends headed into the school courtyard. "Hey—good morning!" he said, reaching out an index finger and sliding it lightly through Becca's hair. "Ready for another year?"

"When have you known Becca *not* to be ready?" Tyler asked. "I bet she mapped out our whole year for us on the ride to school."

Becca laughed with the others, a little embarrassed, but not much. She sometimes worried about being too pushy—although usually by the time she started worrying, it was too late. But she liked being a person with ideas and enthusiasm. Looking around at her friends, she knew they liked that about her too—most of the time, at least.

"Whatcha planning this time, Dreamer?" Nate asked her. She liked *that* about *him*—that he could see the dreamer side of her. Most people thought dreaming and being a doer didn't go together, but Nate knew better.

"Brio Bible study," she said promptly. "We gotta get it going right away, don't you think?" She included all the friends in the question.

"When shall we meet—Fridays after school?" Jacie suggested.

"Not this week—we've got the Edge leadership retreat Friday night," Hannah reminded them. All of them but Solana, who wasn't active in a church youth group, were signed up for the retreat for Christian student leaders.

"How about Thursdays?" Nate said. "That won't conflict with sports."

"And it's close enough to the weekend that people are ready to kick back for a while after school," added Tyler.

"Sounds good to me," Becca said. "Jacie? Solana? Hannah?"

The girls nodded, and Hannah said, "Think we can pull it together by this Thursday, or is that too soon?"

"Sure we can," Becca said. "I'll send an e-mail to everyone who came last year, and we can put posters up as soon as Jacie can get them done."

"Were you going to ask her first?" Tyler said.

"Who?"

"Jacie. Were you going to ask her if she *wants* to make posters?"

"Oh." Becca paused blankly for a second, then caught on. "*Oh!* Right. Uh, Jacie, would you make posters advertising the Brio Bible study?"

"Of course," Jacie said. "But thanks for asking."

"And I'll make sure to ask Kara to come," Becca said, as much to herself as to the others. "We'll have to get Mr. Girard to okay our using a room, and decide what we're going to talk about for the first meeting, and . . . Wow—we're going to have a *lot* to talk about over lunch."

Tyler laughed. "That's our Becca. Always about three hours ahead of herself. How about we start the day by going to first hour? Mine's this way." He waved and jogged off down the math-and-science wing. Solana followed him.

"I have to go to the newspaper office," Hannah said. "See you at lunch."

"And I'm off to art class. *Finally!*" Jacie said. "Thank goodness they managed to hire enough teachers to open all the sections."

"I'm going to stop by my locker first," Becca told Nate. "I want to make sure I can work that lock I had trouble with at registration."

"Just remember to turn right first, then left," Nate said, walking with her to her locker, "not the other way around."

"If only it were so easy," Becca sighed, looking down at her hands. Her difficulty with left and right was a standing joke with her friends, but it had gotten her into trouble more than once. "That's why I told you my combination—just in case I have an especially dyslexic day."

She reached her locker and carefully spun the combination lock. "Ta-da!" she crowed when it swung open. Then, "Awww . . . He's adorable," as she found the plush koala bear clinging to the inside of her locker door with its little magnetic paws.

"My dad brought him back from his last business trip. I asked him to get you something fun from Australia," Nate said.

"Australia has some of the best paragliding in the world," Becca said, tossing the koala gently in the air. "It would be so awesome to go there!"

"I was thinking it might be kind of fun to try paragliding here." Nate pushed Becca's locker shut for her and started toward their first class.

Becca whirled to face Nate and grabbed his arm. "You mean it? You'd go gliding with me? I would love that!"

Nate grinned. "I thought maybe you'd feel that way. So I've been saving up money for a lesson and equipment rental."

"No way!" Becca said. "Your first flight's on me. It'll be my birthday present to you. When shall we go?"

"Well, my birthday's October 10th."

"I'm not waiting that long! Let's go this weekend!" Becca said.

"What about the Edge leadership retreat?"

"Oh, yeah. How about next weekend? Afternoon's the best time for updrafts. Let's go next Saturday afternoon!" Becca was so excited that she scarcely noticed that they were in their first-hour English class. A stifled giggle made her look around. The other students were in their seats, quiet, and looking at her. *Oops,* she thought. *I think I was talking too loud at the wrong time—again.* She shot Nate an apologetic glance and quickly sat down, feeling her cheeks get hot as she made a fuss over arranging her books to avoid making eye contact with Mr. Garner, the English teacher.

To her surprise, Nate continued their conversation in the same loud voice. "So that's settled," he announced, giving Becca a barely perceptible wink. "We'll definitely work on the *first draft* all Saturday afternoon."

Becca stifled a laugh that came out as a sort of strangled snort. *Senior year,* she thought. *It's going to be great!*

● ● ●

The first week of school flashed by for Becca. New classes, old friends, right-up-to-the-last-minute preparations for the Brio Bible study, the excitement of seeing Kara come to Bible study—and before Becca felt she had time to take a deep breath, it was Friday night and she was getting off the bus at Camp Timberline. Milling around her were student leaders from nearly every youth group in the town of Copper Ridge.

"How cool is this?" Tyler said. He and Nate were pulling duffels and sleeping bags out of the cargo compartment of the rented bus and heaving them onto growing piles of luggage. "All these people go to the Edge—but I bet I don't recognize half of them."

"Just think," Hannah said. "We might find some people here from our own school that we didn't even know were Christians!" She looked through her camera to frame a shot, but didn't take one. "Not enough light."

"I don't know why I'm here," Jacie murmured, so softly that Becca almost didn't catch the words.

"What do you mean, Jace?" she asked. "You're here for the same reason as the rest of us: to meet other Christians and get some leadership training."

"Yeah, except everyone else here is a real leader already," Jacie said. She bit her lip and moved toward the shadow of the tall pines as if she'd like to blend in and disappear.

"What are you talking about?" Becca was truly puzzled. Because the Edge was a combined effort of most of the churches in Copper Ridge and was designed to attract teenagers from all the town's high schools, the youth pastors worked hard to get a balance of student leaders from all the different schools. Usually they chose seniors. This was the first time any of the Brio friends had been invited to the leadership retreat. "We've never been leaders before."

"Not at the Edge, maybe," Jacie said, "but you're leaders in your own youth groups." She turned to look at each of the friends in turn. "Hannah plays violin in the church orchestra, Tyler helps choose music for his youth group's praise band, and you—"

"I don't do anything like that," Becca finished for her. "Besides the fact that I'm not musical. I love my youth group, but mostly I just go— I'm not in charge of anything."

"You started the Brio Bible study," Jacie pointed out. "That's leadership.

"So what's your problem, Jacie?" Tyler asked. He flung the last sleeping bag out of the cargo hold and walked over to put his hands on Jacie's shoulders and look her in the eye. "You're telling us you don't belong here because you're not bossy like Becca or a violinist like Hannah or totally hip about music like me?" Even Jacie had to smile at that last comment.

Becca ignored Tyler's jab about bossiness. She knew what was bugging Jacie now. "You know, Jacie," she said, "you may be right. Oh, sure you got Damien out of his shell with that little painting thing you did—"

"That *little* painting thing that won first prize in the county art show?" Nate interrupted. Becca flashed him a smile that came and went so fast, he probably didn't even see it in the dark. Nate was quick—he'd already figured out what she was doing.

"That's the one," Becca agreed. "Sure, now Damien's coming to the Edge every month and getting involved in church, but I can see why Jacie wouldn't really say she showed *leadership*."

"And on the missions trip in Venezuela," Hannah said, "she *did* manage to break through the language barrier when she illustrated the gospel using sidewalk chalk. And it's true that a whole lot of children committed their lives to Christ. But I can see why she wouldn't call *that* leadership."

"And of course, she came up with the idea of a slave sale *and* brought in the top bid when we were raising money for Dragonfly Ranch," Tyler said. "But you're right—I can see why Jacie would say she's not really a leader."

"Help me out here," Nate said. "Why *would* Jacie say she's not a leader?"

"Because she's INSANE!" screamed Becca, diving at Jacie to wrap her in a hug.

"Group hug!" yelled Tyler, throwing his arms around Jacie and Becca. Nate wrapped his long arms as far around them as he could reach, and before Becca really knew what was happening, the people around them were dropping their bags, taking up the call "Group hug!" and piling into the jumble of arms and bodies.

● ● ●

"This is a team-building challenge," the camp staffer told the group assembled at the challenge course on Saturday morning. "So there's no right or wrong way to do it. All that matters is that you work together to accomplish it."

Becca looked around as the facilitator—he'd introduced himself as Tito—went over basic safety rules. Ponderosa pines towered above them. Straight as telephone poles, bare trunks stretched 20, 30, some as high as 45 feet before branches grew out from the grooved, cinnamon-colored bark. From one of the high branches a thick rope hung nearly to the forest floor. Becca tipped her head back and looked up at the sky beyond the green branches. When she squinted her eyes, the light filtering through the long needles danced and rippled through a fishnet of blue-green shadows. *It's almost like being underwater,* she thought.

Tito finished the safety rules and began to explain the first challenge. "A terrorist cell has unleashed a deadly virus. The only vaccine is locked in this safe—" he tapped a short, hollow log, "on this island." Tito dragged a stick through the dirt to draw a circle around the "safe."

"Pretty small for an island," Tyler murmured.

Tito nodded. "Yep. Pretty small. But you have to get your entire team on it because the safe is programmed to open only when it senses the simultaneous fingerprints of 18 different people—the exact number in your team. But that's not all."

He drew a larger circle around the island. "The island is protected by this 10-foot moat filled with radioactive material. You touch the moat, you die. Oh—and fingerprints from a dead person won't activate the safe."

The team waited for Tito to continue.

"That's it," he said. "Now it's up to you."

Becca's eyes sparkled. A challenge! That's what she loved. The rope she'd noticed earlier hung on the other side of the "island." They could use the rope to swing across the "moat" and onto the island. Everyone else must have had the same idea at about the same time, because they moved in a mass around the edge of the moat to get to the rope. But it hung out of reach, closer to the island than to their edge of the moat.

"This is a team challenge, right? So we have to think like a team." The guy who spoke up lifted his hands in a shrug. "What do we have together that we don't have individually?"

"Long arms," said a petite girl, pointing at Nate and giggling.

"Thanks, uh—what's your name?" said the guy who asked for ideas.

"Amanda," the girl said.

"Thanks, Amanda. My name's Jake." Jake grinned at Nate. "So let's try it with the long arms."

Nate reached for the rope, but it was beyond even his grasp.

"Nice try. Anybody got any other ideas?" With Jake as their unofficial leader, the team tried one thing after another. They tried throwing things at the rope from the other side, trying to make it swing closer to the reaching team. They tried picking up Nate and holding him horizontally; that didn't work at all. Becca found a stick, but she couldn't catch the rope with it.

"Somebody find a stick with a bend at the end," she said. "I bet I could hook the rope then."

The ground was covered with a thick carpet of pine needles and little twigs, but not with long sticks with bends in the end.

"Tell you what," Jake said, sitting down on the ground. "Let's try this." He pushed up one leg of his long, baggy shorts and unclasped an artificial leg.

For a long moment, the group just stood there.

Jake looked up at his stupefied team members. Gesturing with the prosthetic leg, he said, "Don't worry about it. I don't." His mouth twisted up in a kind of half smile that looked as much resigned as amused.

He probably gets this kind of reaction a lot, Becca thought. *People think he's just another ordinary guy, and then they're stunned when they realize he has a fake leg. I'd hate that.* She tried to look casual, as if people took their legs off around her every day. But she felt phony. *Just don't look freaked out,* she told herself. *That's probably the main thing.*

Deliberately, she tore her gaze off Jake's leg and looked instead at his eyes. The smile he gave this time was full and genuine. "Here," he said. "See if you can reach it with this." Then he handed her the leg.

chapter 7

Just don't look freaked out, Becca repeated to herself. To Jake she said, "Do you mean. . . ?"

"Go ahead," Jake encouraged. "See if you can hook the rope with it."

Gingerly Becca grasped one end—the non-foot end—of the prosthesis. It was lighter than she expected, but even so she was worried about losing her grip and dropping it. She would have to hold it in just one hand if she was going to reach as far as possible. She glanced at Jake and he gave her an encouraging nod. She leaned over the moat and stretched toward the rope.

She got tantalizingly close, but still she was an inch or so short. She leaned out as far as she dared, and Nate held her hips to steady her. This time the shoe on the prosthetic leg nudged the rope, setting it swinging.

"Almost got it," Becca called without taking her eyes off the rope.

"Go for it, Becca!"

"You can do it!"

With her teammates cheering her on, Becca strained to reach just a little farther. Leaning forward, she got the foot to the rope, just past the rope, then behind the rope.

"Yea! You got it!" cheered her team. But as Becca drew the rope toward them, it slipped over the rounded toe of the shoe and swung away.

"Ohhh!" moaned the team.

Frowning in concentration, Becca went after the rope again. But now that it was swinging, it was harder to reach. Becca thought about giving Jake's leg to someone with longer arms—Nate, maybe—but she wasn't sure about the etiquette of the situation. Was it acceptable to pass around parts of another person's body without permission? She decided to give it another try herself. She nearly hooked the rope, but again it swung just out of reach.

"I wish you had a longer leg," she said to Jake, then clamped her free hand to her mouth, horrified at what she had just said. Everything and everyone suddenly seemed to get very still.

"And I wish you had longer arms," Jake said, and to Becca's relief he laughed. "Here, give me my leg," he added.

Taking the prosthesis from Becca, he sat right at the edge of the moat. "Hold on to me," he said, and half a dozen of his teammates held him steady. Jake leaned so far forward that he was nearly lying flat. With the prosthetic foot he hooked the rope and pulled it within reach. Becca grabbed it and the team went wild. "Whoa, Jake! Way to go!"

As guys slapped Jake on the back, he quickly strapped his leg back on and stood up. "Who's going over first?" he asked.

● ● ●

The camp bell rang, signaling lunchtime, just as the group got the final member onto the "island." They erupted into cheers when Tito gave them a thumbs-up.

"That was a blast!" Becca said to Jacie and Hannah as they climbed the hill to the dining hall. "I bet Tito never had a team solve the challenge like that before."

"Wasn't it creepy touching Jake's leg, though?" Jacie asked in a low voice. "I'm sure I would have freaked out if he'd handed it to me."

"That's what I kept telling myself—'don't freak out,'" Becca admitted. "But Jake was really cool about it, don't you think? He made me think of my life verse: 'I can do all things through Christ who gives me strength.'"

"That's a good verse," Hannah said. "It sounds like you."

"Thanks!" Becca couldn't think of a better compliment than that. And hearing it from Hannah, who took Scripture as seriously as anyone Becca knew, made it even more meaningful. "I hope it describes senior year for me," she confided.

"Today will definitely be one of your unforgettable memories from senior year," Hannah said. "I just wish I'd thought to take a picture to capture the look on your face when Jake handed you his leg!"

"Solana's going to die when we tell her," Jacie said. "I wish she could be here this weekend."

"Me, too," Becca said. "You know who else I wish could be here? Ricky and Gina. A team's challenge like that would be so cool for them! I bet even Ricky and Gina could learn to get along if they were working together on something like that."

"Why not bring them here?" Hannah asked.

Becca stood still and gaped at Hannah. "You're a genius!" she said. "Why didn't I think of that? This place is perfect!"

"This place is expensive," Jacie reminded her. "Don't forget what our registration fee cost."

"Could the Community Center pay the cost for the kids?" Hannah suggested.

"Uh-uh." Becca shook her head decisively. "No money for extras in the budget at the Community Center. But I'm sure we can find people to help with finances. Shoot, it's such a good cause maybe the camp will let the kids come for free!"

"I wouldn't get your hopes up," Jacie said skeptically.

"But my hopes *are* up! Up, up, up!" Becca said, jumping to shoot an imaginary basketball. She grinned at Jacie. "Don't forget: I can do all things through Christ who gives me strength!"

● ● ●

Tito had the high ropes course scheduled for Saturday afternoon's activity. Becca, Nate, and Tyler were so eager to try it that they dragged Jacie and Hannah to the course as soon as they had swallowed their last bites of tomato soup and grilled-cheese sandwiches. The camp facilitators were getting the course ready: checking cable connections and laying out safety harnesses. One of the guys brushed past Becca with an armload of helmets, then stopped and did a double take. "Hey, Brown Eyes!" he said to Becca. "Remember me?"

No, thought Becca, *but I bet I should*. He looked familiar, but she couldn't remember where she knew him from. She considered brushing it off with the standard, two-syllable "Hey-ey" that people use when they can't remember somebody's name, but she decided that could get awkward if they kept running into each other over the weekend. *Besides*, she realized, *he doesn't remember my name either. I mean—Brown Eyes?* Shrugging, she said, "Help me out."

"Danny. From Copper Mountain," he said, naming the ski slope where Becca usually went paragliding in the off-season.

"Oh! The gondola guy!" Becca remembered. He'd been running the lift the day Otis's paraglider crashed; the accident had driven pretty much everything else about that day out of her mind. "Do you know what happened to Otis—the guy who crashed? Have you heard anything about him?"

"Nah. I took a job here for the summer. I don't keep track of gliders."

Becca didn't like how casually Danny treated Otis's accident. Now she recalled that she hadn't much cared for the way Danny had come on to her on the gondola the day she had met him. "Okay. Well," she said, trying to brush Danny off, "we'll get out of your way here."

"You're never in the way, Brown Eyes," Danny said as Becca moved purposefully away. Tyler snickered and Becca shrugged apologetically at Nate.

"Ooh, Brown Eyes, you're never in *my* way," Tyler cooed. "Better watch out for this guy, Nate. His is a subtlety women can't resist."

Becca slugged him in the arm, and Tyler cried, "Oh, Brown Eyes, you're hurting me!"

Before Becca could think of a way to retaliate, Tito called out, "Teams! Gather at the ropes course!" The people straggling down the trail from the dining hall picked up their pace and joined them at the course.

"This morning you learned to work as a team," Tito reminded them. "Now you're going to have to trust those team members with your safety rope as you accomplish some personal challenges. We call this 'challenge by choice,'" he explained. "No one will force you to do anything you don't want to do. But we will encourage you to challenge yourself as much as you feel ready for." He pointed to a platform attached 35 feet up on the trunk of a ponderosa pine. "For some of you, that may mean simply climbing to the first platform."

Tyler reached over and gave Jacie a squeeze around the shoulders. Becca caught her eye and smiled encouragingly. The friends all knew how terrified Jacie was of heights—the first platform would be a major accomplishment for her. "You can do it, Jace," she whispered.

"And if you don't," Hannah added, "that's okay, too. Like Tito says, it's your choice."

Jacie nibbled her lip, her eyes wide as they took in the platform. She nodded.

"Just watch for a while," Tyler suggested. "Then you can decide if you want to try it."

The facilitators handed out safety harnesses and helmets. Becca saw Danny coming her way and suspected he was going to try to help adjust the webbing of her harness, but it was so similar to her paragliding gear that she had it in place and tightened before he reached her.

"Quick work, Brown Eyes," Tyler whispered with a grin. "Danny," he called aloud, "can you show me how to hook *my* harness?" Danny gave him a disgusted look and walked away.

Tito went over the commands and safety rules, and at last they were ready to go. Becca was one of the first to volunteer. She scrambled up to the platform and clipped her carabiner to the cable above her head. Her safety rope ran from her harness, through the carabiner, and down to the ground where Jake held it taut to catch her if she fell.

"On belay!" Becca called out.

"Belay on," Jake responded.

Unlike Jacie, Becca loved the thrill of heights. The sense of risk she got as she prepared to step off the platform gave her an adrenaline rush. The first challenge was to cross a Burma bridge—a cable strung between two ponderosas. Two horizontal ropes about waist-high served as handrails.

It looked easier than it was, Becca quickly realized. The rope handrails were slack and swayed when she put any weight on them. Maintaining her balance while she was standing still was challenge enough; when she tried to walk, she set the whole contraption swinging. Looking at the cable under her feet, Becca's focus shifted to the ground below. "Thirty-five feet is a lot higher from up here than it is from down there," she called down.

"Trust the rope, Becca," Tito called back. "If you fall, you won't go 35 feet—only about 35 inches. At least, if Jake does his job!"

"Here goes nothing!" Slowly, as steadily as she could, Becca shifted all her weight to her left foot. Carefully she picked up her right foot and placed it ahead of her left on the cable.

"Way to go, Becca!" The cheers from her teammates made it sound as if Becca had just won a marathon instead of taking one tiny step. Emboldened, Becca took a second, then a third.

"Hey! You didn't tell us it gets harder toward the middle!" she called. The cable swayed beneath her feet and Becca tried to compensate by leaning first one way, then the other. "Aaiiyee!" she yelled as she lost her balance and fell off the cable. Instinctively, she squeezed her eyes shut.

"Gotcha!" At the sound of Jake's calm voice, Becca opened her eyes. Tito was right: She'd dropped only about three feet before Jake's grip on her safety rope had stopped her fall.

"Now what?" she asked Tito.

"Get back on the cable." To the group on the ground, Becca heard him say more quietly, "This should be fun to watch."

The cable was about level with Becca's waist but, with nothing to brace her feet against, climbing onto it was a real challenge. Becca lost count of how many times she slipped off the cable to hang by her harness. By the time she finally got on her feet, she realized that her fear of falling was gone. With increased confidence she seemed to have gained increased balance, and she crossed the Burma bridge with only one more fall.

"Now clip onto the zip line," Tito told her when she reached the platform at the end of the Burma bridge. Becca hooked her carabiner onto the pulley system at the top of a cable that went down toward the ground. "This is your elevator down," Tito said. "Just sit back in your harness. Ready for a ride?"

"Ready!" Becca stepped off the platform and soared down the cable. "Wheeee! I'm flying!" At the bottom, she said, "Can I do that again?"

The afternoon sped away as Becca and the others mastered the challenges Tito had for them on the high ropes. By the end of the day, they were clowning around on the cables as if they were on the ground. Tyler did a surfer boy routine on the Burma bridge while Nate and Jake played Hacky Sack on another part of the course. Becca even tried a handstand—and fell off immediately. Hannah, who always said she was uncoordinated, had such success when she was paired with a partner that she and her partner went through the course three times. Only Jacie stayed on the ground.

"All right, guys—last call!" Tito checked his watch. "Anybody want one more turn? Or anybody who hasn't gone want to try it?" He looked at Jacie, and the rest of the group did, too.

Jacie fidgeted with the safety harness. "I don't know."

"It's your choice," Tito said. "But I'm going to encourage you to climb a little way up the pole here." He put his hand on the pegs that served as climbing rungs. "Why don't you give it a try and see how far you can go?" He turned to the rest of the group. "Team? Will you encourage Jacie if she wants to try it?"

The group erupted in cheers and applause, but Jacie still looked uncertain. Then Jake said, "Tell you what, Jacie. If you want to try, I'll give you a leg up."

Becca got the joke first and burst into a sputter of laughter. Jacie smiled at Jake—a small upturn of the mouth first, growing into a genuine, double-dimple smile.

She took a deep breath and bit her bottom lip. She tilted her head way back to look up the pole, then back at Jake. "Okay, I'll try," she said, her voice barely audible. "But you can keep your leg," she said, her smile returning. "I'll have enough trouble with my own two wobbly ones."

Jacie hooked her harness to the climbing rope and slowly started up the pole.

"Go, Jacie! You can do it," Becca yelled with the others. *Just like Alvaro*, she thought. At that moment she imagined Gina putting on the harness instead of Jacie.

Jacie put her foot in Jake's cupped hands and stepped up to the first rung. She climbed slowly but steadily up to the platform. When she got there, she stood, clinging to the tree trunk.

"Good job, Jacie!" Tito yelled, and the team applauded. "Do you want to try the Burma bridge?"

Silently, Jacie shook her head.

"Want to climb down?"

Again, Jacie shook her head.

"Okay. You want to stand there a while getting the feel of it?"

"No." Jacie's voice was thin and quavery. "I want to come down."

"That's okay. Just climb back down."

Jacie looked at the pegs on the tree trunk. Because of the way the platform extended, the pegs were on the opposite side of the trunk from the platform. To get to them required a big step without much to hold on to. "I can't." Her voice rose hysterically. "I can't! I'm stuck!"

c h a p t e r 8

"You're not stuck, Jacie," Tito encouraged. "Just one big step, and then it's like coming down a ladder. I've got you on belay—trust the rope."

"I can't," Jacie repeated. "I'd rather go down the zip line."

"But the zip line is across the Burma bridge," Tito said. "Do you want to try crossing the bridge?"

"No!" From the way Jacie's voice shook, Becca was afraid she was close to tears.

Tito looked at Danny. "Plan B?"

"Plan B," Danny agreed. He strapped himself into a harness and swarmed up the tree to the platform where Jacie stood. "How about if I help you climb down?"

Jacie squeezed her eyes shut and shook her head. "I'm sorry. I can't."

Danny looked down at Tito, and Tito nodded.

"You still want to try the zip line?" Danny asked Jacie. When she nodded, he said, "Do you trust me to carry you over there?"

Eyes still tightly closed, Jacie nodded again. Danny clipped his carabiner and Jacie's onto the safety cable, quietly explaining to Jacie what he was doing. After a little coaxing, Jacie released her grip on the tree trunk and wrapped her arms tightly around Danny's neck. As the hushed team below watched, Danny crossed the cable with Jacie in his arms. He transferred both their carabiners to the zip line and brought her safely to the ground.

The team burst into applause and cheers. *Maybe I misjudged Danny,* Becca thought. *Maybe he really isn't a jerk.*

Danny escorted Jacie to the waiting team. As he passed Becca, he whispered in her ear, "I'd like to do that with you, Brown Eyes."

Jerk.

● ● ●

"You go on without me." Jacie turned over on her bottom bunk to face the wall.

"Jacie! You can't miss tonight's meeting." Becca clambered onto the bunk and pushed her face between Jacie's and the wall. "Tomorrow we go home. This is the last chance to be together with everybody."

"I don't want to be with everybody. I feel totally, completely stupid. I humiliated myself on the ropes today."

Becca started to deny it, but stopped. *Nobody thinks Jacie is stupid. But Jacie will never believe me if I say that.*

"I think I know how you feel." Hannah sat on the edge of Jacie's bunk and the metal frame creaked in protest. "Remember on the missions trip when I went through an entire performance with that embarrassing stain on the back of my skirt?"

"That was different. You couldn't help that your period started early," Jacie said.

"But it was still humiliating. Everybody laughed at me. Nobody laughed at you today, Jacie," Hannah said.

"Probably because they all felt sorry for me." Jacie pulled her pillow over her face, blocking out Becca and Hannah.

Becca yanked the pillow off Jacie's face. "The only one feeling sorry for you is you. So get over it." She saw a flicker of anger in Jacie's eyes. But Jacie was never angry for very long, and almost at once her expression changed to teasing.

"You sure know how to sympathize, don't you, Becca?" Jacie said.

"It's called tough love," Becca answered. "So, okay—we love you. Can we go to the meeting now?"

"Only if we can sit in the back. And if somebody brings it up I'm leaving."

"Deal."

When the three girls opened the door to the main lodge, Becca felt Jacie hang back. So instead of finding a place toward the front of the group gathering in a semicircle around the fireplace, Becca steered Jacie and Hannah to one of the couches near the perimeter. She and Hannah sat protectively on either side of Jacie. Jake spotted them and came over to sit on the arm of the couch, and then Tyler squeezed himself in between Hannah and Jacie, draping his arms around both of them. Nate sat on the floor and leaned back against Becca's legs.

During opening devotions, Becca felt Jacie slowly relax, and by the time students started talking about what the weekend had meant to them, Jacie was leaning forward to listen as eagerly as anyone. Then Lisa, a girl from their team, stood up.

"I learned a lot from all you guys," she said, looking around at the group. "But the person who helped me the most is Jacie." She turned to talk directly to Jacie. "I was pretty scared about a lot of the challenges today. And to tell you the truth, watching people who found it easy didn't help much."

Oops, thought Becca. *That would be me.*

"But Jacie, you tried something that was really hard for you," Lisa continued. "Maybe it didn't turn out the way you hoped, but it really made me think. I don't like to try something if I don't think I'll be able to do it—and do it well. That's one reason I don't always live the way I know Christ wants me to. It's too hard. And sometimes it's scary." Lisa looked around the room. "I want to make a pledge in front of you all that from now on I'm going to take the challenge to live completely for Christ."

When the applause died down, Jacie stood up. "I learned something today too," she began softly. "Sometimes I think of my faith as trusting Christianity—sort of like trusting the rope when you're up on the cable. But really, being a Christian is trusting a *person*—trusting Jesus to take me in His arms and carry me when I can't do anything on my own." She sat down.

"Well done," Tyler told Jacie. He leaned across to talk to Becca. "But I bet that's the first time anybody's compared Danny to Jesus."

chapter

DEAR GOD,

WHAT AN AWESOME WEEKEND THIS HAS BEEN! YOU'VE TAUGHT ME SO MUCH! I CAN'T WAIT TO SHARE AN EXPERIENCE LIKE THIS WITH GINA AND RICKY AND THE OTHER KIDS AT THE COMMUNITY CENTER. GOD, PLEASE HELP ME GET AN ADVENTURE PROGRAM LIKE THIS STARTED FOR THEM. AND THEN USE IT TO GIVE KIDS LIKE RICKY THE COURAGE TO FACE THE THINGS THAT SCARE THEM, AND TO HELP GINA LEARN TO TRUST YOU.

YOURS FOREVER,
BECCA

P.S. I'LL TALK TO MRS. R. ABOUT STARTING AN ADVENTURE PROGRAM WHEN I GO TO THE CENTER ON FRIDAY. COULD YOU PLEASE WORK ON HER BEFORE THEN SO SHE'LL SAY YES?

● ● ●

Becca stood in front of her friends at the school lunch table, twisting her napkin. "We can't get together to hang out this Friday night."

The Brios and Nate groaned. "Come on, Becca," Solana pleaded. "It's the only night I can be with Ramón."

"It's my first overnight shift at the Community Center homeless shelter," she explained. "And I want to go in early to talk with Mrs. Robeson about starting an adventure program for the Center." She paused, looking at Solana. "Unless you really mind."

"'Course not! This adventure camp idea is important," Tyler said.

"I guess Ramón and I can do something with the others. If anybody can convince Mrs. Robeson, you can," Solana added. "The way you've talked about Camp Timberline all week, you've got me ready to sign up!"

"Show her the pictures Hannah took of the camp," Jacie suggested. "She'll be more interested if she can see what it's like."

"I'll make copies you can give her to keep," Hannah promised. "And we'll pray for you too, won't we, guys?"

When they were alone Becca asked Nate, "Sure you don't mind?"

"No. You need to talk with Mrs. R. Do you want me to come in later to keep you company on the night shift?"

"I'd love it!" Becca said. "But I don't think Mrs. Robeson would. And I need to prove that I'm responsible if she's going to let me start this program."

Nate nodded. "That's okay. We'll have all Saturday afternoon together. If I don't get killed on my first attempt at paragliding!"

Friday after school Becca put the things she thought she'd need for the night at the shelter in her school backpack, had supper with her family, and then went to Outreach Community Center. Tapping on the door of Mrs. Robeson's office, she felt both nervous and excited. *Help me say this right, God*, she prayed silently, her eyes squeezed shut. *If this is what You want for Ricky and Gina, please let Mrs. Robeson say yes.*

"Yes," Mrs. Robeson said, and Becca's eyes popped open.

Wow! That was fast!

"What can I do for you, Becca?"

"You can let me start an adventure program," Becca blurted out, forgetting her carefully prepared speech. Eagerly, she told Mrs. Robeson all about her conversations with Ricky and Gina, her experiences climbing with Alvaro and on the Edge retreat, and her conviction that an adventure program could help Ricky, Gina, and the other kids at the Community Center.

When Becca finally paused for breath Mrs. Robeson said, "Come in and sit down, Becca." Seating herself behind her desk, Mrs. Robeson leaned forward and studied the camp photos that Becca laid out for her. "Let me get this clear: Are you talking about a field trip to this camp, or something more?"

"More," Becca said firmly. "I'd like to kick off the program with an overnight at Camp Timberline, because having a good block of time like that will really set the course of the program. But if it's just a one-time thing, that's not enough. I think we need an adventure program that's an ongoing part of the Community Center, just like the rec program is. The adventure program wouldn't meet every day, of course, but maybe once a month."

Mrs. Robeson pulled out a notepad and began to write. "Give me an idea of the kinds of things you envision the children doing," she said.

Becca was ready with a long list of ideas for all seasons. "And best of all," she concluded, "everything we do with the kids can point them to Jesus." She told Mrs. Robeson what Jacie said in the fireside meeting at the retreat. "Well," she said at last, "what do you think?"

"I think it's an idea with real potential," Mrs. Robeson said. "But—the Community Center has no funds and no staffing available to launch or maintain another program."

"I know. But what if I could find the funds? And what if I got it going as a volunteer?" Becca responded. "That's what I want to do."

"Are you sure you can take on a project of this magnitude?" Mrs.

Robeson asked. "I can't release you from your commitment to the homeless shelter to give you time to work on this, you know. I need you there to keep that ministry going."

"I wasn't going to ask to quit," Becca assured her. "I would do both. I'm sure I can. 'I can do all things through Christ who gives me strength'," she quoted.

"Indeed," said Mrs. Robeson dryly. "Have you read that verse in context? I have always understood it to mean that God will give us the strength to handle any circumstance He sends us, not that He endorses unlimited activity."

"But God *did* send this idea," Becca countered. "And He opened a door when I went to Camp Timberline. I really believe that."

"Then you had better keep going until you find a closed door," Mrs. Robeson said. "Just be aware that you have many more doors to get through before this dream of yours is a reality. I don't want you to have false hopes about this being easy."

"You mean it's okay? You'll let me do it?" Becca could hardly believe it.

"No one would be happier than I to see an adventure program here at Outreach Community Center," Mrs. Robeson said, with a smile that made Becca sit straighter and feel prouder. "You know, of course, that it will have to meet the same requirements for safety, insurance, and accountability as the other programs. I'll put together a file of the relevant information before I go home and leave it for you in the workroom." She gestured to the adjoining office.

"Thanks, Mrs. R.! I'll have plenty of time to go over it tonight." Becca laughed. "I've got all night!"

Before Becca could sit down and work on her plans for the adventure program, though, she had work to do at the homeless shelter. Not that it felt like work. She loved talking with the people at the shelter, especially the kids. In particular, she wanted to check in with Ricky and see how sleeping on the men's side was working out.

"It's all right," Ricky said when she asked him, but he didn't sound convinced. "None of the crazies jumped me yet."

"I guess it takes courage to move to the adult side," Becca said. She hoped if she told Ricky he was brave, he might *feel* brave. She wasn't lying, either; she did think it took courage. "Want to hear a story about courage? Something that happened on a retreat I was on last week?"

"I don't care," Ricky said, but he looked interested, so Becca told him about Camp Timberline. He laughed out loud when she told him about Jake and his leg, and he pored over the pictures Becca pulled out of her backpack.

"This looks like a real cool place," he said.

"It is," Becca agreed. "How'd you like to go there sometime?"

"Don't be funning me, Becca. I ain't going to no camp."

"Don't be so sure," Becca told him. "I've got a plan. I'm going to start an adventure program here at the Center, and you can be in it. At least," she teased, "if you think you're brave enough to try those high ropes."

"What you talking about *brave?*" Ricky said, puffing out his chest. "Ain't I just told you how I'm sleeping on the grown-up side now? Ain't you just said that's brave? Darn right I'm brave!"

"Darn right!" Becca said, giving him a high five. *And you better believe I'm going to make this happen for you,* she added silently.

"What else you got in that backpack?" Ricky asked, dumping the contents out.

"Homework, toothbrush, journal, Uno cards," Becca began itemizing the stuff she'd brought along.

"Let's play Uno!" Ricky grabbed the cards.

"Sure. Ask Gina if she wants to play too."

"Aw, do I gotta?" Ricky protested.

"Not if you're scared she'll beat you," Becca said slyly.

"Gina! Get over here!"

● ● ●

Not until the lights were out and the shelter was quiet for the night did Becca get a chance to look at the file Mrs. Robeson had left for her. Kicking her shoes off and sitting cross-legged in the orange-upholstered office chair, she eagerly spread the contents of the file folder on the computer desk in the workroom. Mrs. R. wasn't kidding when she said there were a lot of requirements to meet. Becca flipped through the information, making mental notes as she went.

1) *Insurance—that will take money. Parent/guardian permission and medical release forms—that's easy—Mrs. R. included a form to copy.*

2) *Transportation—who knew that drivers had to have a commercial vehicle license and special mountain training? Guess carting the kids in the family Suburban is out.*

3) *Program goals—Mrs. R.'s personal requirement.*

Becca looked over the list and decided to start writing program goals. That, at least, she had clear in her mind. Some of the other things—insurance, transportation, and above all the money to fund them with—she'd have to do a little research on.

Becca powered up the computer and created a new folder: Adventure Program. It looked so official. After a couple of drafts, Becca had the program goals just the way she wanted them. She printed out a copy and slid it under Mrs. Robeson's office door. A glance at the clock on the computer toolbar showed that it was already 2:00 A.M.

She was too geared up to sleep, but she was feeling hungry, so she padded, silent in her stocking feet, into the kitchen. She didn't want to turn on a light and risk waking anyone in the shelter room, so she groped her way to the refrigerator and opened the door. The refrigerator light cast a dim glow over the near end of the kitchen, and Becca made a quick inventory of the pantry shelves: spaghetti sauce—industrial-sized can; applesauce—also industrial-sized; pancake mix—50 pounds; canned pudding—120 servings; 15 loaves of bread.

Becca sighed. No chips, no cookies. And she didn't think opening a 120-serving can of pudding for her midnight snack would be a real good idea. She turned her attention to the refrigerator. There she found the unappealing leftovers of Friday night's supper, several gallons of milk, two 10-pound blocks of cheese, and a stack of packages of soft flour tortillas.

Cheese tortillas it is, Becca decided. She flipped a light on long enough to find a sharp knife and carve off a couple chunks of cheese. She wrapped them in cold tortillas and padded back to the workroom, munching as she went. *Nothing like Mama Luz's crispy fried tortillas,* she thought, mentally savoring the meals she often ate at Solana's house. *But this will do.*

Back in the workroom, she opened a new file and started a to-do list:

1) *Call Camp Timberline about weekend availability. Target: last weekend in October. Discuss donating time/facilities or providing at a discount.* That would give her the maximum time to get everything lined up before the weather got too cold.
2) *Call insurance company.* She pulled Mrs. Robeson's notes out of the folder and copied down the name of the insurance company the Community Center used, as well as the number of their current policy.
3) *Find out how to get money!!!!!*

Becca looked a long time at the last item on her list. Money was definitely going to be the biggest challenge. For all her big talk about finding funding, she really didn't have the slightest idea how to go about it.

I'll ask Mom in the morning, she decided. *She gets funding for the Center all the time. She'll know what to do.*

Becca put her head down on the desk for a quick rest before starting on her homework. Her arm rested on the keybozzzzzzzzzzzzzzzzzzzzzzzzzzz

chapter 10

Becca stirred. Her mouth tasted of cheese, and she didn't even want to think about what her breath smelled like. For the first time, she was glad she wasn't going to be serving breakfast in the homeless shelter. Her shift officially ended before breakfast, and she was going home to take a shower—and brush her teeth!

She looked over her to-do list. Except for the mystery line of zzzz's at the bottom, she thought she could probably accomplish everything before Nate came to pick her up at one. She printed the list on the back of a piece of used paper—Outreach Community Center recycled everything possible—and shut down the computer.

On her way out, she stopped to say good-bye to Ricky and Gina. They were lined up outside the bathrooms, waiting their turn for the too-few showers. *We really* need more space, Becca realized for about the hundredth time. *What's it going to take to get through to that zoning board?*

At home, Becca's phone calls took longer than she expected. The insurance agent who worked with Outreach Community Center's account was with another client when she called. So she left her name and phone number, along with the account number of the Community Center's policy, in exchange for the promise of a return call. "Our office closes at noon on Saturdays," the receptionist told her. "I'll try to have Mr. Zuiderveldt return your call before he leaves—but I can't guarantee that he'll be able to do so."

She didn't get even that far on her first call to Camp Timberline. The answering machine she reached assured her that the staff was busy with campers on the weekends but that her call would be returned as soon as possible on Monday.

"I can't wait till Monday," Becca told the machine. "I really need to talk to somebody about using the camp on the last weekend of October." She began explaining the adventure program until a beep sounded and the machine cut her off. *Crud! And I didn't get to leave my number!* Becca realized. She punched "Redial" on her phone, but the line was busy. Several tries later, she finally connected and left her name and number with an urgent request that someone call her back as soon as possible.

I'm not getting very far on this list, she thought. *I haven't checked off a single thing yet.* She put her pen at the last item on the list: *Find out how to get money.* "Mom!" she yelled. "Can I talk to you?"

At least Mrs. McKinnon had time to give Becca the information she needed. In her work as part-time administrator at Outreach Community Center, Mrs. McKinnon had researched nearly every funding possibility for programs working with children.

"A grant is your best bet," she advised. "There's no way you can raise the kind of money you need with bake sales and car washes."

Becca agreed. She and her friends had held just about every fund-raiser conceivable over the summer, trying to raise money for Solana's family ranch. She knew what a slow process that could be. Besides, she and her friends were pretty well fund-raised out.

Mrs. McKinnon got on the Internet and helped Becca find organizations offering grant money, and showed her what to look for among those available.

"You want a renewable grant if you can get one," Mrs. McKinnon said, "because otherwise you have to find funding all over again next year. But more important for you right now is finding one that has a timeframe that works for you."

"What do you mean?" Becca asked.

"Here's an example," her mom said, going to a Web site called *Friends of the Children.* "This foundation offers grants to organizations that benefit children."

"Perfect!" Becca took the mouse from her mom and scrolled down the screen, skimming the requirements. "This is exactly what I'm looking for!"

"Have you read this part yet?" her mom asked, pointing to a paragraph headed "Grant-Making Cycles."

"Next application deadline: September 15th," Becca read aloud. She looked at the calendar. "Wow! That's next week! That'll be really tight, but I think I can do it."

"Keep reading," said her mother.

"Grant notification: December 15th. *December!*" Becca yelped. "They won't even decide until December?"

"Right. And then there may be another delay before the money is distributed."

"But I need the money by the end of October," Becca said. "I practically promised Ricky he'd get to go to Camp Timberline, and if we don't go in October it'll be too cold to use the challenge course till spring. Ricky needs this program before spring!"

"That may not be possible, Becca," her mom said gently.

"It has to be," Becca said. "Anyway, I'm not giving up till I'm absolutely, utterly convinced that it's impossible." *I can do all things . . .* she reminded herself.

"That's my girl! I feel the same way when I'm fighting for something," Mrs. McKinnon said.

"Like the zoning for the homeless shelter?"

"Exactly! I won't take no for an answer until I'm sure it's God's answer," Mrs. McKinnon said. "And so far I'm not convinced."

"Me, neither. About not getting a grant, I mean," Becca said. "I'll just keep looking till I find one that will work."

After what seemed like hours, Becca had looked at Web sites for more foundations and organizations than she would have guessed existed. But she still hadn't found anything that was likely to give her a grant by the end of October. The application deadlines were long past for the ones who distributed money in October. Others had no deadlines, but took seven or eight months from proposal to funding. Nearly all of them had lengthy and intimidating application forms.

Becca was getting discouraged. She had set three tasks for herself for the morning, and she hadn't accomplished a single one. Halfheartedly, she went to the next Web site on her list.

"Grants are reviewed on an ongoing basis," she read. "You will be informed of the Trust's decision within three months of the date that the proposal is received. Under special circumstances, distribution of funds can be accomplished in less time."

Yes! Becca thought. *This is it! Thank You, God!*

Quickly she scrolled to the application form. The introductory paragraph advised her, "A brief letter of inquiry, rather than a fully developed proposal, is an advisable first step for an applicant."

A brief letter of inquiry—Becca could do that, and it wouldn't take nearly as long as filling out the entire application. In her letter she could explain why it was so important that she get the grant quickly.

"Mom!" she yelled. "I think I found one!" She bookmarked the site, then hurried through the house to find her mom. In the family room, she noticed Kassy, lying on her back on the big, overstuffed couch, talking on the phone.

"Kassy," Becca said, "I'm waiting for an important phone call."

"Shh!" Kassy flapped a hand at Becca signaling her to go away, then clamped her hand over her ear. "Shut *up!*" she said to the person on the other end of the phone. "Did he really say that? What did she say to him?"

"Kassy," Becca tried again.

"Hang on a minute," Kassy said into the phone. She explained to Becca, "Lydia says Justin VanderVeen told Carissa to tell Alli that he likes me! I never even guessed!"

Becca sorted that one out for a moment. "Who's Justin VanderVeen? Wait—never mind. I'm expecting an important phone call. Do you think you could call Lydia back later?"

Kassy rolled her eyes. "We *have* Call Waiting, Becca."

"So have any calls come in for me?"

"I've got to get back to Lydia," Kassy said evasively.

"Kassy!" Becca grabbed the phone from her sister. "I'm hanging up on Lydia right now unless you promise that you'll pick up any calls that come in." She poised her thumb threateningly over the "Off" button.

"Fine," huffed Kassy. "Now give me back the phone."

"Promise?" Becca persisted.

"Promise."

Becca relinquished the phone and went to find her mom, who was fixing a peanut-butter and banana sandwich for Alvaro in the kitchen. While Becca was describing the grant, Kassy yelled from the family room.

"Becca! Phone call from Camp Timberline!"

"I got it!" Becca raced to take the phone from Kassy. "Hello?"

"Hey, Brown Eyes! Guess who?" said the voice on the other end.

Oh, no! Becca thought. *Of all the people to call me back.* Aloud she said, "Danny, right? Hey, can you let me talk to somebody about reserving the camp?"

Becca was still on the phone when Nate arrived. He came in through the kitchen door, and she heard him teasing Alvaro and talking with her mother.

"Where's Becca?" he asked after a few minutes.

"She's on the phone with some guy named Danny," Kassy answered.

"Danny! Not that guy from the camp! How did he get her number?" Nate sounded annoyed.

"She gave it to him, I guess," Kassy said.

Becca carried the phone into the kitchen. "It's Camp Timberline," she explained to Nate, her hand over the mouthpiece. "I'm trying to set up something for the adventure program."

"Great!" A smile replaced the frown on Nate's face. "So Mrs. Robeson gave you the go-ahead?"

Becca nodded, then motioned for him to shush. "Uh-huh," she said into the receiver. "Yeah, I could come up to the camp. Monday? Okay, but it'll have to be after school. Right. I'll be there."

Hanging up the phone, she turned to Nate and her mom. "Great news! Camp Timberline has the last weekend in October open! I need to go there and work out the details, but they're willing to rent the place for cheaper if we provide our own staff."

She picked up the phone again. "I've got to call the Brios! Wouldn't it rock for all of us to be facilitators for the challenge course?"

"I'm not sure it would be so much fun for Jacie," Nate chuckled.

"Oh! Right!" Becca paused in her dialing. "But she can be a counselor and she'll be awesome with the kids." She finished dialing and waited for Jacie to pick up the phone. "Jacie," she said, "I've got the best news!"

chapter 11

"Why are you looking so cheerful on a Monday?" Solana demanded as Becca put her lunch tray on their usual table in the quad. "That's just wrong."

"You'd be cheerful too, if you had the kind of weekend I had," Becca said.

"Aha! A hot date with Nate," Solana said knowingly.

"That's not what I'm talking about," Becca said with a laugh.

"Gee. Thanks a lot," Nate said.

"Get used to it, man," Tyler said. "That's women for you. You risk your life paragliding, and they turn around and tell you you're nothing special."

"That's right! You went paragliding Saturday. How was it?" Jacie asked.

"It was cool. Way cool," Nate said. "Words can't describe how cool."

"That never stops Becca from trying," Tyler teased.

"Was Otis there?" Hannah asked. Becca gave her a grateful smile.

She'd told her friends about Otis way last spring when he had his accident, and by the way Hannah periodically asked about him, she knew Hannah hadn't forgotten her promise to pray for him.

"No, he wasn't there," Becca said. "I asked around, but nobody's seen him. Somebody heard he was in rehab somewhere, but they didn't know where."

"Too bad!" Jacie said. "But you had a good time anyway? Tell us all about it, Nate! Was it scary?"

"You would have been scared, I think," Nate said. "It's definitely not for anybody who's afraid of heights."

"That reminds me, Jacie," Becca said. "I was thinking you could be a facilitator for the low teams course—the challenges on the ground."

"In the adventure program, you mean?"

"Yeah. I definitely want Christians for the staff, so we don't end up with Danny or anybody like him," Becca said.

"So I guess that lets me out?" Solana said. Becca didn't know what to answer; she hadn't thought about excluding Solana, but it was true that Solana didn't even claim to be a Christian.

Into the silence Hannah said, "Maybe this is the time you'll decide you want to make a commitment to Christ, Solana." She smiled and poked Solana in the ribs.

"Or maybe not," Solana replied, whacking her with the back of her hand.

"Maybe Solana and I could work together," Jacie suggested. "She could do the physical part of the ropes course, and I could do the debriefing and the part where we tie it to our spiritual lives. It's just a thought," she added. "It would be more fun if we could all be there together."

"You'd love this place, Sol," Tyler said. "They have horses there, too. Would horseback riding be part of the adventure program, Becca?"

"Yeah—that would be great! I was wondering what we'd do with the kids who are too small for the ropes course."

They were still talking excitedly about ideas for the adventure program when the bell rang.

"Oh, Nate!" Jacie said. "We never got to hear about your paragliding."

"Why don't we go to Copperchino after school?" Tyler suggested. "Nate, you can give us a blow-by-blow report of paragliding. Get it?" He nudged Jacie. "Blow by blow?"

Everybody groaned, but they agreed to meet at the coffeehouse.

"I can't," Becca said. "I have to go to Camp Timberline today." Normally she'd feel bad about missing out on time with her friends, but she was eager to work out the details of the adventure program with the camp—even if it might mean fending off Danny's advances again.

"We could go to Copperchino tomorrow instead," Nate said.

Becca shook her head. "I've got to go straight home tomorrow in case the insurance company calls me back. Plus I've got to start making calls to bus companies about transportation. It's hard to catch people during office hours when you're in school all day."

"Wednesday?" Jacie suggested.

"I don't know—it depends on whether I have to make more phone calls. Listen, don't change your plans for me. I guess this is just going to be a busy week," Becca said. "But we'll get together at my house for sure on Friday, okay? Yes," she added before Solana could ask. "Ramón's invited too."

● ● ●

On Thursday evening Becca burst into the kitchen. "Sorry I'm late, Mom. I stayed after Bible study to talk to Kara."

"That's okay. We just sat down to pray," Mrs. McKinnon answered.

"Pray for Kara, will you, Dad?" Becca dropped her backpack in the corner and sat at her place at the table. "She's asking a lot of questions about Jesus and Christianity."

After Mr. McKinnon asked a blessing on the meal, Kassy asked, "Kara? Isn't she the girl who was into Wicca?"

"Mm-hmm," Becca said around a mouthful of spaghetti. "She started coming to the Brio Bible study last spring. I think she's really searching." Becca wiped her mouth with a napkin. "We're going to get together one-on-one to talk about God."

"Jesus is God," Alvaro said.

The rest of the family beamed at him. "That's right, Alvaro. Jesus *is* God," Mr. McKinnon said. "And He loves you very much."

"I love Him too. More pasketti, please."

Becca felt a wave of affection for Alvaro wash over her. Even with his face covered with spaghetti sauce, he was adorable. And his young faith was so secure. She knew her parents had a lot to do with that. *They've done such a good job teaching all of us about Jesus,* she thought. *And it never seems preachy—because their faith is so real.*

"I'm a little worried that Kara will have questions I can't answer," Becca admitted to her parents. "Do you think you could help me if I get stuck?"

"Of course," her mother said. "But it's more important for you to be honest with Kara than for you to have all the answers."

Mr. McKinnon agreed. "If she asks you something you're not sure about, it's okay to tell her you don't know, but that you'll try to find out."

That made sense to Becca. "I guess I thought I'd have to cram before Kara and I get together. I wonder if there's time to meet with her tomorrow before the Brios come over."

"Far be it from me to say that housework is more important than discipleship," Becca's mom said, "but have you looked in the family room lately?"

"Why?" Becca asked.

"Because the rest of us have been tripping over your stacks of paper all week," Mrs. McKinnon said.

"That's my stuff for the adventure program," Becca explained. "Paperwork from Camp Timberline, brochures from bus companies, information on grant proposals. I need all that stuff."

"Then you'll probably want to get it organized and filed before your friends come over Friday night," Mr. McKinnon said. "You'll be pretty sorry if anything important gets lost."

Becca saw his point. "I'll work on it right after supper," she said.

"No fair!" Kassy complained. "Mom, are you going to let Becca get out of cleaning up the dishes *again?* I've done it every night this week! And I've tucked Alvaro in bed, too."

"I want Becca tonight," Alvaro said. "I want Cat in Hat Come Back."

"But I've got an English essay to finish," Becca said. "If I have to clean up the kitchen and tuck Alvaro in bed, I won't have time to set up files, too."

Kassy crossed her arms and met Becca's eyes in a stubborn stare. Alvaro clapped his hands and singsonged, "Cat in hat come back! Becca read me Cat in Hat Come Back!" Becca looked at her mother, but Mrs. McKinnon just raised her eyebrows as if to say, "What do *you* think you should do?" Mr. McKinnon was no help at all; he was serving himself a second helping of spaghetti as if the matter of evening chores were already settled.

"Fine," Becca said. "I'll do the kitchen chores and tuck Alvaro in bed tonight, and I'll clear away my piles in the family room tomorrow after school. Kara and I can get together sometime next week, I guess."

Alvaro slid off his booster seat and ran over to Becca. He planted a tomato-ey kiss on her cheek and promised, *"I'll* read to *you*, Becca. I can read Cat in Hat Come Back very good. I can read it with the book upside down!"

● ● ●

Sorting her papers into files was more work than Becca anticipated, and she was glad she hadn't tried to squeeze in a meeting with Kara after all. She had barely gotten everything organized in the heavy cardboard box her dad had given her, when her friends arrived.

"Take a look at this," she said, taking Nate by the hand and dragging him to admire her color-coded, neatly labeled file folders. "Impressive, huh?"

"Scary," Tyler said. "What are you becoming, some kind of Junior Achievement type?"

"Hey! Don't knock Junior Achievement!" Solana grabbed the front of Tyler's shirt. "Or 4-H, either. Some of us are proud of accomplishing things instead of just playing around." She took a good look at Becca's file box. "Although I have to say the fuchsia folders are a little more Martha Stewart than I care for."

"I think it's wonderful," Jacie told Becca. "They're just jealous because they've never been organized in their lives."

"And proud of it," Tyler proclaimed, leaping onto the couch and landing on his back with a squashy thump.

But Solana was not about to take the insult lying down. "Not organized! You're saying I'm not organized? Excuse me, but you are talking to the youngest intern ever to work for The Greenhouse Conservancy. I didn't get that job by being disorganized!"

"Do you ever work on grant proposals for the conservancy?" Becca asked Solana. "Because I have this giant proposal to pull together by October 1st."

"That's less than three weeks away. I don't know a lot about grants, but I know that's not very long to write a good proposal," Solana said.

"I know, but that's when it's due," Becca said. "I sent a letter of inquiry and the foundation e-mailed me back today. They said they'll review my proposal right away, but I have to get it in by October 1st."

"What would the grant cover?" Jacie asked.

Nate and Ramon wandered over to the DVD rack and Tyler got off the couch to join them in flipping through the movies, so Becca picked up her file box and sat down on the couch.

"If this program is going to get off the ground, I'll need the grant to pay for insurance, camp fees, transportation, and supplies." Becca flipped through her folders to see if she'd forgotten anything. "I'm not sure yet what that will cost, but I think we'll have to rely on volunteers for staff."

Tyler looked up from the DVDs. "That's where we come in. High ropes facilitators extraordinaire!" He struck what he clearly imagined to be a heroic pose, and the girls all laughed.

"Actually," Becca said, "I have some bad news about that. When I went to the camp on Monday I found out that facilitators have to be at least 21."

"What?!" Tyler exclaimed. "That stinks!"

"I'll say," Nate said. "I thought it was all set that we were going to handle the ropes course."

"You've got to be kidding, Becca!" Solana flipped her black hair with an angry motion. "You could at least have found that out before you recruited us."

"I'm sorry," Becca said. "I didn't know there was an age requirement until I went to the camp on Monday. I'm just as disappointed as you are."

"Hey, it's okay," Nate said. He sat next to Becca on the couch and smoothed a stray lock of hair out of her eyes. "Don't worry about it."

"It's just that there are so many details to keep track of," Becca explained. "I'm still learning what questions to ask—that's why I didn't think about an age requirement."

"Hey, like the man said—don't worry about it," Tyler said. "So, are we going to watch a movie tonight or what?"

"I was thinking maybe we could pick out what team challenges to have the kids do for the adventure program," Becca said, pulling a pamphlet out of her Camp Timberline folder. "I have descriptions right here . . ."

Solana pulled a cushion from the couch and threw it at Becca, Nate took the file box and shoved it behind the couch, and Tyler put a DVD in the player and turned the volume up high.

"Or . . . we could watch a movie," Becca said.

chapter 12

"How did Monday get here so fast?" Becca muttered to herself as she spun the combination on her locker. A big yawn broke her concentration. "Shoot! Did I just do 32 left, or 14 right?"

"'Morning, Becca." Jacie was all sunshine and smiles, and Becca groaned. "Ready for the physics test this afternoon?"

"I'll be lucky not to sleep through it," Becca said. "I did the night shift at the homeless shelter on Saturday, and I stayed up late last night working on the grant proposal. You wouldn't believe all the information they need! They want financial statements showing what percentage of the funds will go to administration, what percentage will directly benefit the kids, and all kinds of stuff. I have to work up a whole budget before I can even do the grant proposal. But before I can work up a budget, I have to get estimates on insurance and transportation, figure out what equipment we'll need to buy and how much it will cost . . ."

Jacie shook her head in commiseration. "It makes me tired just thinking about it."

"Me, too," Becca said, giving her lock a final twist and opening her locker. "All I really want to do is work with the kids." A parchment-colored piece of paper fluttered from her locker to the floor.

"What's that?" Jacie asked as Becca stooped to retrieve the paper.

"Looks like a gift certificate. Oh, wait—it's homemade." Becca read it aloud: *"Need a lift? This certificate good for one fully caffeinated grande mochaccino at Copperchino. Offer good today after school.* It's from Nate!"

"Awww, that is so sweet," Jacie said. "I've got to find a guy like that to take care of me."

"Don't let Solana catch you talking like that," Becca warned, "or you'll get a lecture on how women can take care of themselves. But it is nice to have somebody treat you like you're special," she admitted.

"It works both ways," Jacie pointed out. "Nate thought it was pretty special that you took him paragliding."

"It was an early birthday present," Becca said. "But we ought to do something on his actual birthday. Nate told me his dad's going to be in Australia again, so they're not going to celebrate as a family till he gets back."

"An 18th birthday is too important not to celebrate," Jacie said decisively. "We should give him a party. Not just a get-together-and-hangout party; something that really kicks."

"His birthday's on a Friday, too, so that's perfect," Becca said.

"Should it be a surprise?" Jacie asked.

Becca thought for a moment. "No, let's tell him about it. I think he's kind of bummed about his dad being gone so much, and this will give him something to look forward to."

"Want to get together tomorrow with Hannah and Solana and make some plans?" Jacie suggested. "I have to work at six, but I'm free right after school."

"Yeah! We could meet in Old Town and grab an early supper together before you go to work."

"Perfect! I haven't gone out to supper in forever, and there's a new Vietnamese restaurant I've been wanting to try." Jacie glanced at the hall clock. "I've got to go—I want to do a little work on the adventure pro-gram logo before class starts, and there's an oil pastel in just the shade I want in the studio."

As Jacie walked away, Kara approached hesitantly. "Hi, Becca," she said, in the soft voice that seemed to be her trademark. Kara always seemed a little unsure of herself and how people would respond to her, which made Becca want to go out of her way to be warm and friendly.

"Hi, Kara," she responded. She gave Kara her full attention. "How was your weekend?"

"Fine." Kara's eyes widened in a hopeful expression. "Do you think we can get together sometime this week?"

"I'd love to!" Becca's enthusiasm was genuine. "When works for you?"

"Well, I work every evening, but after school any day is fine," Kara said. "Today would work."

"Oh, shoot—I can't do it today." Becca looked at the gift certificate from Nate. "Another friend already asked me to do something. And I just made plans for tomorrow, too."

"Wednesday, then?" Kara suggested.

"I'm supposed to watch my little brother after school," Becca said, "but I'll see if my sister will do it."

"Okay." Kara gave one of her shy smiles. "I'm looking forward to it. I really want to hear more about what you think about the difference between Wicca and Christianity."

Becca sent up a silent but jubilant prayer. *Thank You, God! Now give me the right words to say!*

● ● ●

When Becca got home after her date with Nate, she found a note in Kassy's loopy scrawl at her place at the kitchen table:

Mr. Ciderfelt called—said he'll call tuesday before 5
a bus guy called—call him tuesday by 6

Becca re-read the note. *Mr. Ciderfelt? Who is that?* Puzzled, she said the name out loud. "Oh! Mr. Zuiderveldt—the insurance agent." She needed an estimate from Mr. Zuiderveldt for her grant proposal. How frustrating to miss his call! She glanced at the clock on the kitchen wall. Five minutes to six. Just time to call the bus company back—but which bus company?

"Kassy," she yelled. "Hey, Kass! Where are you?" She walked through the family room and hollered up the stairs. "Kassy? Are you up there?"

"In my room," came the reply, so Becca ran up the stairs to Kassy's bedroom.

"Which bus guy called today?" she asked.

"Huh?" Kassy looked up from the *Brio* magazine she was reading.

"What bus company?" Becca repeated, holding up Kassy's note.

"Oh. I didn't get the name. I figured you'd know."

"Kassy, I've called at least seven bus companies. How am I supposed to know which one to call back?"

Kassy just shrugged. "Call 'em all, I guess."

"Are you kidding? Do you know how long that takes?" In a mechanical voice, she mimicked, "If you are calling about an existing account, press 1 . . ."

"Well sor-ry! I'm not your private secretary, you know!" Kassy rolled over on her bed and returned to her magazine, leaving Becca to glare at her back.

"Some help she is," Becca muttered as she pounded down the stairs. "I guess now wouldn't be the time to ask her to watch Alvaro for me." She picked up the phone and glanced again at the clock. 6:01. She dialed rapidly and got an answering machine.

"Jace? It's Becca. Listen, I'm sorry, but I can't go to Old Town tomorrow after all. I've got to be home for some phone calls. Can you come to my house instead?"

Becca hung up the phone. She felt bad about gypping Jacie out of supper at the Vietnamese restaurant, but she didn't see what else she could do. *I guess I'll have to call all seven bus companies and leave messages on all their answering machines.*

She took the bus file from her file box and dialed the first company on her list. *If you are calling from a Touch-Tone phone, please press . . .*

● ● ●

"Have some cookies," Becca said, dumping the contents of a half-empty bag of Chips Ahoy! on a plate.

"Store-bought?" Solana picked up a cookie to inspect it. "Does anybody really eat these things?"

"Baking takes time," Becca pointed out. "And nobody here seems to have much of that lately."

"Plus your mom doesn't believe that food equals love, the way my mama does," Solana said. She nibbled the edge of the cookie. "Not bad. It almost tastes like food."

"You're spoiled, Sol." Jacie bit into a cookie and talked around the crumbs. "Having your mom home all the time. You, too." She pointed her cookie at Hannah. "My mom and I *live* on convenience food. If you nuke these, the chocolate gets all gooey and they're almost like fresh-baked."

"Great idea!" Becca put the plate in the microwave and punched instructions into the keypad. "Okay, so no Chips Ahoy! for Nate's party. What if we—" The phone rang and Becca grabbed the cordless handset. "I'll take it in the family room; that's where my files are."

About 10 minutes later she finished the call and went back in the kitchen. "Bus company," she explained, "calling with an estimate."

Jacie nodded. "So about Nate's party . . ."

"Hey! What happened to those cookies?" Solana demanded.

"Oops. I got distracted when the phone rang and forgot to get them out of the microwave." Becca got up from the table.

"But the microwave is still running," Jacie said. "How long did you set it for?"

"Fifty seconds," Becca said. "Oh, no! I set it for 50 *minutes!*" She hit the "Stop" button and pulled the plate out. Melted chocolate bubbled and congealed on the plate, and a smell of scorched chocolate filled the kitchen.

"Maybe they'll still *taste* okay," Hannah said in a doubtful voice.

Becca blew on a cookie until it was cool enough to try. The texture was what she imagined you'd get if you stirred gravel into bubble gum. "Wow—who would have thought a cookie could be stretchy and crunchy at the same time?"

"Make a note," Solana said. "Becca does not bake the cake for the party."

"I'll bake the cake," Hannah volunteered. "I've got a great recipe we used for the twins' last birthday."

The phone rang again and Becca shrugged apologetically. "Sorry. Don't wait for me—you can fill me in on what you decide when I'm done with this call." She pushed the "Talk" button and went into the family room. When she got back, Hannah pushed a sheet of notebook paper across the table to her.

"We figured the food wasn't all that important to you," she stole a quick glance at the plate of mutant cookies, "so we decided what to serve. Solana and I will take care of the homemade stuff, and you can buy the rest."

"Thanks," Becca said gratefully. "The only things I'm really good at making are frozen pizza, mac and cheese from a box, and fried tortillas."

"We have to decide what we're going to *do* at the party," Solana said.

"What does Nate like?" Hannah asked.

"Becca," Jacie answered promptly.

"Okay, so we put Becca in the cake . . ." Solana began.

"Solana!" Becca and Hannah cried in unison. Solana smiled her naughtiest smile.

"Nate likes sports," Becca said. "And almost any kind of competition."

"So we could try to rent a gym, or play volleyball in the backyard, or go to a climbing wall—" Solana said.

"You can go to a climbing wall," Jacie put in. "I'll stay back and arrange cookies on a platter."

"Or we could make a tournament of birthday party games," Hannah said. "You know—the kind little kids play. Like Pin the Tail on the Donkey."

"And those paddles with the ball on the elastic," Jacie said. "I stink at those."

"And three-legged races. We'll pair Hannah with a really hot guy," Solana teased.

"A little kid's party for turning 18," Becca considered, tapping her pen on the table. "It could either be really fun or really lame. What do you think?"

"I don't know," Solana said. "We just did that for Alvaro's birthday."

Before anyone had time to comment, the phone rang again. "Sorry," Becca mouthed and again took the call in the other room. It was Mr. Zuiderveldt from the insurance agency, and the conversation took a long time. By the time Becca had finished explaining as accurately as possible what the adventure program would entail, the ages of the participants, and the relationship of the program to the Community Center, Jacie had her car keys out and was standing at the door.

"I've got to run, Becca," she said. "I'll design the invitations and get them to you to send out, okay?"

"That would be great! Thanks, Jacie!" Becca said.

"I've got to go too," Hannah said. "I wrote down everything we decided."

"Would you like to stay for supper?" Becca asked. "My mom won't mind."

"Thanks, but our family always eats together," Hannah said. "I'd better go home."

"I'll pass too," Solana said, eyeing the molten cookie mass.

"Well, thanks for coming up with all the party ideas," Becca said, just as the phone rang again. "Oops—gotta get that. See you tomorrow!"

chapter 13

WEDNESDAY, SEPT. 15

DEAR GOD,

I BLEW IT TODAY. I TOTALLY FORGOT TO ASK KASSY TO WATCH ALVARO AFTER SCHOOL, SO I COULDN'T TAKE KARA OUT FOR COFFEE LIKE I PLANNED. AND I COULDN'T HAVE HER COME HOME WITH ME, BECAUSE BETWEEN ALVARO WANTING ME TO PLAY WITH HIM AND THE PHONE RINGING ALL THE TIME, NOBODY CAN HAVE A DECENT CONVERSATION.

ONCE I GET EVERYTHING SORTED OUT SO I CAN WRITE THE GRANT PROPOSAL, THINGS WILL BE BETTER. WILL YOU PLEASE HELP ME WITH THAT? BECAUSE THE PROPOSAL IS DUE TWO WEEKS FROM TODAY!

THURSDAY, SEPT. 16

DEAR GOD,

Kara DIDN'T SEEM MAD AT ME WHEN I SAW HER IN BIBLE STUDY. THANKS FOR THAT! DIDN'T HAVE TIME TO TALK WITH HER AFTERWARD, THOUGH—MR. GARNER ASSIGNED A TON OF READING FOR TOMORROW AND I'M ALREADY BEHIND.

FRIDAY

GOT A CALL THAT I HAD TO GO TO CAMP TIMBERLINE TODAY ABOUT SOME GLITCH IN THE PAPERWORK. HAD TO TELL THE BROS THEY COULDN'T COME OVER TONIGHT—SOLANA WAS TICKED. WHAT AM I SUPPOSED TO DO—DROP THE ADVENTURE PROGRAM SO SHE CAN HANG AT MY HOUSE WITH RAMON?

WORKING WITH DANNY AT CAMP IS REALLY GETTING ON MY NERVES. NO WAY CAN I USE HIM AS A FACILITATOR. BUT TITO IS BACK AT COLLEGE, AND WE'RE ALL TOO YOUNG. WHO?

SUNDAY

FORGOT TO TAKE MY JOURNAL TO THE HOMELESS SHELTER SATURDAY NIGHT, SO DIDN'T WRITE. SPENT TIME ON THE GRANT PROPOSAL INSTEAD. DIDN'T SEE NATE AT ALL THIS WEEKEND. ' NO MORE TIME TO WRITE NOW.

TUESDAY

NO TIME TO WRITE.

● ● ●

"You're blowing us off again?" Solana spun on her heel as if to stalk out of the school courtyard, but apparently decided she had more to say, and came back. "You might try applying some of your own sermons to yourself."

"What are you talking about?" Becca looked around at the rest of her friends, bewildered. "All I said was we couldn't get together at my house tonight after all."

"Yeah—for the third Friday in a month!" Solana shot back. "Remember how you got on my case for ignoring my friends when I first started seeing so much of Ramón? Well, it's payback time, sister. I'm calling you on it."

"But this is different, Solana," Becca explained. "I *can't* hang out with you tonight—Danny called yesterday to tell me I have to enter all this information into their database—names and addresses of the kids who'll be in the adventure program, guardian information, stuff like that."

"Why can't you just e-mail it to them?" Jacie said. "You could do that from home in less than a quarter of the time it takes to travel to camp and back."

"I have to do the data entry myself; that's part of the deal I worked with the camp. I provide all the manpower and the activities, and they give me a discount on using the facilities," Becca said.

"And you can't do data entry via e-mail," Nate explained in response to Jacie's puzzled expression. "It's a different format." Becca gave his hand a grateful squeeze for being so understanding.

"If you're providing all the activities, why do you even have to bother with their database?" Hannah asked.

Becca shrugged. "Insurance. Certification. There's so much red tape in this whole process, you wouldn't believe it."

"So let dear old Danny cool his heels till tomorrow," Tyler said. "He doesn't have to have that data tonight; he's just trying to get you up there in the dark."

"Knock it off, Tyler! I don't like seeing him any more than you do." Becca linked her arm in Nate's to emphasize her point. "But somebody has to show me how to use the program, and nobody's available on Saturday because they have a group coming up for the day. All the staff will be busy."

"Yeah, like *you're* always busy," Solana said. "Too busy for your friends."

"Come on, that's not fair!" Becca searched her memory for a good example to prove that she was making time for her friends. It was true that she'd been canceling Fridays at her house, but surely she'd done other things with her friends lately. *Coffee at Copperchino? No—I guess I've bailed on that the last few times. I haven't gone since I went with Nate . . .* She couldn't really remember when it was that she went out with all her friends after school. *But Sol and Jacie and Hannah were over at my house a week ago—well, a week and a half ago.* She squelched the memory of how she had reneged on her suggestion of going out for supper the night they made plans for Nate's party.

"Okay—I *have* been really busy lately," she admitted. "But there's so much to get done . . ." Solana raised her eyebrows and Becca decided not to try to defend herself. "But honestly, I *am* spending time with you guys. Or at least I'm going to. Like Nate's party—we'll have an awesome time together."

"Have you heard from anybody yet?" Jacie asked. "How many people are coming?"

Becca looked blankly at Jacie, then it hit her. *The invitations!* She had never even addressed them, much less mailed them. She tried to think how she could have forgotten something that important. *Jacie gave them to me—when? Last week? That's when I was so busy getting all the financial figures for the grant proposal. And then I started working on writing the proposal . . .*

Her dismay must have shown in her face, because Jacie said, "What's the matter? Was there something wrong with them? You didn't like them!"

"No—no. They're great," Becca said. Her forced enthusiasm didn't sound convincing even to herself.

"She didn't mail them," Solana guessed.

That was the worst thing about having a best friend, Becca thought; you could never fool her. Shamefacedly, Becca nodded.

"I worked really hard to get those done so you could mail them in plenty of time!" Jacie looked mad, but even worse, she looked hurt. "Now people won't even know about the party and they'll make other plans for that night!"

"I'm sorry, Jacie," Becca said. She truly meant it. Right now she'd give a lot to go back in time and take care of those invitations. But it was too late. "I'll call everybody as soon as I get my grant proposal turned in. It's due Wednesday," she calculated out loud, "and I can call everybody Thursday. That still gives people over a week's notice."

"You mean you let Jacie do all that work for nothing?" Tyler said. "That's really low, Becca. If Jacie made the invitations, you ought to use them."

"But I have no time!" Becca said. "I've got to go to the camp tonight and volunteer at the shelter on Saturday, and I still have tons to do on the proposal. If I don't get that in by Wednesday, I don't get the money for the adventure program."

Jacie looked miserable. Becca felt like a heel, but she decided to sacrifice her pride a little more in the hope that she could salvage the invitations for Jacie's sake. "Would . . . would you guys take care of mailing the invitations?"

Tyler made a disgusted sound, but when he looked at Jacie's face, he bit back whatever he had been about to say. Becca saw him exchange a glance with Solana, nodding just slightly toward Jacie.

"Fine," Solana snapped. "We'll send out your invitations. We may as well; we've done everything else for this party so far." Solana shook her head. "I'm sorry, Becca. You helped me so much with *Tío* Manuel's ranch. I really have no right to begrudge you a few minutes addressing invitations."

"Why don't you give them to us now, Becca," Hannah said. She didn't act mad, just patient, which was almost as bad. "We'll address them and get them in the mail this evening."

"They're at home," Becca said in a tiny voice. "Can you go pick them up?"

● ● ●

I'll make it up to them, Becca told herself on the drive home from Camp Timberline late that night. *Nate's party will be really special, and we'll all have a great time. And then we'll launch the adventure program, and the Brios will see that it really was worth spending all this time on.* She was exhausted, physically and emotionally, from the confrontation with her friends, and then from spending an hour and a half hunched over a keyboard inputting data. But she had to admit that Danny was a good teacher. He'd even showed her some shortcuts that saved her a lot of time. Otherwise she'd be heading home on dark mountain roads even later than she was.

Kassy's bedroom window glowed when Becca pulled into the driveway, but the rest of the house was dark. She let herself in quietly and tiptoed upstairs. On impulse, she went into Alvaro's room. He looked very small and vulnerable in the illumination of his nightlight. He had kicked all his covers into a tangle, so Becca straightened them out and smoothed them over him. As she tucked him in snugly, she saw that he was clutching his battered copy of *The Cat in the Hat Comes Back*—the special book Becca read to him whenever she tucked him in.

At least Alvaro still loves me.

She tiptoed out and almost screamed. "Kassy," she gasped, "you scared me half to death standing in the shadows like that."

"Yeah, well *you* scared *me* half to death prowling around in the dark like that!" Kassy whispered.

"I was just checking on Alvaro," Becca said. In the dark, her smile warmed her voice. "He's sleeping with *The Cat in the Hat Comes Back*."

"Yeah. I read that to him when I tucked him in tonight," said Kassy.

Becca felt as if someone had knocked the wind out of her. "*You* read it to him? That's *our* special book—Alvaro's and mine!"

"Well, you haven't exactly been around to read it to him, have you?" Kassy drifted back to her room and closed the door.

c h a p t e r 14

Work to be done. Work to be done. The refrain ran through Becca's head as she filled in the final section of the grant application form. *Finished at last!* she thought as she turned the page over with a flourish—only to see yet another page to be completed.

As she picked up the new page, a gust of wind blew through the window, rustling the completed pages. A second gust lifted them from the desk. As Becca reached for them, the walls melted and the pages soared out of reach. Becca ran after them, and ran and ran and ran. Just as she was about to catch them, an avalanche of pink snow buried the papers.

Becca was frantically digging when the Cat in the Hat appeared, wearing a prosthetic leg. "Help me shovel the snow," Becca pleaded. The cat took off his hat, and there, standing on his head, was Alvaro. "Help me, Alvaro!" Becca cried, but Alvaro jumped down into Kassy's arms.

"We're going to a party with Solana," Kassy said. "Jacie sent us an invitation."

"Wait for me!" Becca started to rush after them, but the cat hooked her shoulder with his artificial leg. Becca tried to shake him off, but the leg clung to her shoulder.

"Becca, wake up." Mrs. McKinnon shook Becca's shoulder a little harder. "Did you forget the training session at the Community Center today?"

Becca opened her eyes and blinked to clear away the traces of her dream. "What training session?"

"With the firefighters," her mom reminded her. "For staff and volunteers at the Center, remember?"

Becca groaned. "Shoot! I was going to work on the grant proposal today."

Mrs. McKinnon gave Becca the kind of scrutiny that always made her feel as if she were in the doctor's examining room. "You look worn out," she pronounced, feeling Becca's forehead with the back of her hand. "Maybe I should call Mrs. Robeson and tell her you can't make the training session."

Becca sat up. "I'm fine! And I can't skip the session—I signed up for it; they're counting on me."

Mrs. McKinnon sat down on the edge of the bed. "You've signed up for kind of a lot lately, haven't you? I hate to see you so overcommitted that you run yourself ragged."

"I'm fine," Becca repeated. "Really."

Mrs. McKinnon shook her head. "Look at your life, Becca. Up late at the camp Friday night, up early Saturday morning to go to the Community Center. Work all Saturday night at the homeless shelter and rush home in time for church. You're running from one thing to the next like a mad woman. And in the meantime, you're hardly even seeing your family or your friends. Do you really believe you're fine?"

"Okay—I'm a little extra busy right now," Becca acknowledged, "but once I get this grant proposal turned in on Wednesday, things will slow down."

"So you're just going crazy till Wednesday? Will it be any different on Thursday? Or will you be just as busy then catching up on the things you put off doing in your rush to finish the proposal?"

Becca realized that's exactly what she had planned to do when she offered to call Nate's party guests on Thursday. Her friends had taken that job off her back, but she still had schoolwork hanging over her head, as well as plenty to do on the adventure program. She slumped against her pillow. Just thinking about all she had to do was overwhelming. But what choice did she have?

"Oh, Honey!" Her mom reached out to smooth Becca's hair, the way she used to do when Becca was a little girl. "You need to find some balance in your life. Right now you remind me of the beginning of that book you always read to Alvaro. You know the one I mean?"

How could she forget? She even remembered it in her dreams. Becca recited the opening lines of *The Cat in the Hat Comes Back*.

> This was no time for play.
> This was no time for fun.
> This was no time for games.
> There was work to be done.

"Yeah, that's me," she admitted. "But, Mom, I've *got* to do all this stuff. I mean, Mrs. R. needs me at the homeless shelter, and Ricky and Gina *really* need the adventure program, and I *have* to do my schoolwork . . ."

Her mom put a finger to Becca's lips. "I agree that those are all important things. I'm not as certain that *you* need to be the one to do them all. Except your homework," she amended. "But you don't have to save the world all by yourself. Even Jesus had to make choices when He was limited by a human body. He often gave up some opportunities—like teaching big crowds—so that He could take others, like spending time with His disciples."

"But the Bible also says I can do all things through Christ who gives me strength," Becca objected.

"Becca, where is Christ in this when you're neglecting your own little brother and expecting your little sister to take over your responsibilities so you can do great things for other kids?"

Becca didn't answer for a few moments. Her mom's judgment—even though she said it gently—really hurt.

"I would have expected you of all people to understand," she finally muttered. "Look at all you do—family and work and all. I don't see you giving up anything that's important to you."

Her mom raised her eyebrows. "No? Do you remember when Alvaro first came to us? I had to make a choice then."

Becca remembered. Becca had resented Alvaro and the time he took when he came to them as a sickly foster child, and she'd been totally against it when her parents suggested adopting him. So opposed, in fact, that her mom and dad finally gave Alvaro up to another couple.

"But you adopted Alvaro after all," Becca said, recalling the amazing events. "So you didn't really give anything up."

"Yes, we got Alvaro," her mom agreed, a smile lighting her eyes and softening her features. "God is so good! Sometimes He gives us back the very thing we think we have to sacrifice. But giving up Alvaro isn't what I was thinking of," she said. "I was thinking of how I took a leave of absence from work for the rest of the school year so I could be here every day when Alvaro got home from kindergarten."

Becca nodded. At the time she had been amazed that her mom would even consider leaving her work at Outreach Community Center—she loved it so much. But she had told Becca that lots of people could take over her responsibilities at work, but no one could take over her role as Alvaro's mother.

"You're always going to have more opportunities than you can take," Mrs. McKinnon said. "Not just in high school, but for the rest of your life. You have to learn what to take on and when to say no."

Becca nodded, but more to end the conversation than out of agreement. She didn't *disagree* with what her mom said; she just didn't see how any of it could help her right now. She still had a grant proposal to write by Wednesday, and a training session to get to in less than an hour.

● ● ●

"My name is Herb," the firefighter told the staff and volunteers assembled in the multipurpose room at Outreach Community Center. "I inspect this building once a year to make sure it's safe and in compliance with fire codes. Mrs. Robeson invited me to provide some in-service training while I'm here."

Herb wasn't much like Becca's mental picture of a firefighter. For one thing, he was much older. His short-cropped hair was silvery gray, and his dark, bushy eyebrows showed strands of silver too. He had a darkly tanned face crisscrossed with fine lines around the eyes and deep laugh lines around his mouth. He looked as if he was really glad to be talking to them, and Becca decided she was glad he was the officer assigned to them.

First Herb showed them a video demonstrating how to use a hand extinguisher and showing a simulation of an evacuation. Then he walked them through the evacuation plan for Outreach Community Center.

"Your fire alarms are hardwired into your electric system and will ring simultaneously throughout the whole building," he explained. "So wherever you are, you'll hear the alarm, no matter where the fire is. Your system will also alert the fire station. While we're on our way from the station to do our job, your job is to take care of the people in the building."

Herb projected a floor plan of the Community Center onto the screen. "The first thing you do is close all the doors between the fire and where people are. Fire doubles in size every three minutes, and you need to slow it down any way you can.

"Next, take people out the door farthest from the fire." He pointed out the evacuation routes marked on the floor plan. "Never evacuate through another room when you can use a door that leads directly outside," he said. "Smoke has a way of disorienting you, and you may think you're turning left when you're really turning right."

Becca shuddered. She was disoriented about left and right even without smoke. She was glad the room housing the homeless shelter had a door directly to the outside.

"All right; let's go outside for some hands-on practice with an extinguisher," Herb said. He led them to the parking lot, where a fire truck and four more firefighters waited. "This is the rest of my company—Engine 4."

The other firefighters had set up a metal container some distance from the truck. As Becca approached it, she wrinkled her nose.

"Diesel fuel," Herb said, noticing her expression. "Stinks, doesn't it?" He nodded at one of the men in his company, who lit a fuel-soaked rag stuck on the end of a four-foot metal rod. He touched the flaming rag to the diesel fuel in the container and it, too, blazed.

Herb held out a hand extinguisher. "Can I have a volunteer to put this fire out?"

Becca's hand shot into the air, and Herb handed her the extinguisher. "I'll be right behind you with a backup," he said.

Becca took a step toward the fire, but Herb said, "Ah-ah. Don't approach the fire until you're able to extinguish it."

"Sorry," Becca said. She quickly reviewed the procedure she'd seen on the video. She pulled the pin from the extinguisher and grasped the nozzle and then took a step toward the fire.

"That's right," Herb said from behind her. "Now you're ready."

The fire was surprisingly hot for the size of the container. The smoke smelled even worse than the liquid fuel. Becca wasn't sure how close she had to be for the extinguisher to be effective, so she went closer than she wanted to but not so close that she thought she might get burned. Pressing the trigger on the extinguisher, she moved the nozzle in the sweeping motion she had seen on the video. With the first sweep, the fire diminished considerably, and soon it was entirely out.

"Great work!" Herb gripped her shoulder and gave her a look so approving that Becca felt as if she'd done something heroic. "I've never had a first volunteer do such a good job," he said. "Who wants to try next?"

The young firefighter relit the diesel fuel and several other people took turns extinguishing it. By this time, kids were emerging from the Community Center. Becca noticed that Ricky was the first to approach the truck, and Gina wasn't far behind. She walked over to join them.

"No, I can't let you on the truck," one of the firefighters was saying, "but I'll show you what our gear looks like." He let the kids try on helmets and masks.

"Look at me, Becca," Ricky hollered through a face mask. "I wanna be a firefighter when I grow up!"

"You go, Ricky," Becca cheered. She realized it was the first time she'd heard Ricky say anything hopeful about his future.

"If you're going to be a firefighter, you may as well learn how to work the hose," Herb said, joining the crew at the truck. He nodded at one of the other men. "Start the pump and give this young man the booster nozzle."

Ricky eagerly grasped the hose and whooped with delight when water shot out. Becca could tell by the look on his face that he got the idea to squirt Gina, but apparently so could Herb, because he put his strong hand over Ricky's on the nozzle and showed him the proper way to direct the flow. Gina had a turn next, and then every other kid demanded a chance.

By the time the company finally pulled out, sirens blaring, every kid at the Center had a new hero.

"That Herb, he the man!" Ricky told Becca. "I wisht he could come back here some more."

"I don't think Herb's coming back till next year," Becca said, "but how would you like to spend a weekend with guys like Herb?"

"Whaddya mean?"

"I mean guys who will take you on skinny ropes, teach you to climb rocks, and do other kinds of really cool stuff."

Ricky's eyes grew wide. "You mean it?"

"I mean it. Maybe they won't be just like Herb, but they'll know how to do cool stuff and they'll show you how to do it, too."

Ricky popped his chest out and moved about in a circle, his fists pumping the air. "Yeah. *Yeah*. That'd be *real* fine."

Real fine, thought Becca, picturing Ricky at Camp Timberline with strong male role models for a whole weekend. *Real fine*.

chapter 15

Becca dragged herself into school on October 2, exhausted but happy.

"It's done!" she called down the hall as soon as she saw Nate and the others. "My grant proposal is done! I finished it at 11:45 last night and sent it in. Thank goodness for e-mail!"

There was an awkward silence as nobody said anything and Becca realized that her friends didn't share her enthusiasm over meeting her deadline. *I guess they're still mad about Friday*, she thought. To her that seemed ages ago—before the fire in-service training, before hours and hours devoted to making the grant proposal as strong as she possibly could. *But it was really only five days ago*, she realized.

"Can we all go to Copperchino after school to celebrate?" she asked as a peace offering. "My treat."

"Not today," Solana said, and the others shook their heads too.

Becca was stunned. Maybe she'd given them reason to be mad at her by being so busy, but to take revenge by pretending to be too busy themselves—that was just cruel! And childish! Sudden tears stung Becca's eyes, and she angrily blinked them back.

"Fine," she said, trying to keep her voice steady. "I get the message."

"What message?" Tyler said. He looked innocently confused. *Very funny*, Becca thought. *I guess I have to spell it out for you.*

"That you don't want to go for coffee with me."

"Well, no—not when we have Brio Bible study," Nate said. "But tomorrow would be good."

"Brio Bible study!" Becca felt both foolish and incredibly relieved. "That's right—today's Thursday." Unexpectedly, she really did cry. "This is so stupid," she apologized. "I guess I'm just really, really tired."

"Poor thing," Jacie said, giving Becca a hug. Becca looked sharply at her to see if she was being sarcastic, but Jacie's own eyes were moist. *Jacie's so tenderhearted she couldn't even put pins through her bugs for her insect collection in seventh grade*, Becca recalled. *I guess I should know better than to suspect her of holding a grudge.*

"Poor, nothing!" Tyler said, lightening the mood. "Becca's going to be the richest high school senior we know once that grant comes through."

"*If* the grant comes through," Becca said.

"*When* the grant comes through," Tyler corrected. "She's a shoo-in—don't you guys think so?"

"I always thought so," said Solana. "We're talking about Becca, after all."

● ● ●

Becca went through the rest of the day in a haze born partly of sleep-deprivation and partly of euphoria over turning in the grant proposal and making up with her friends. She felt a pang of guilt when she saw Kara at the Brio Bible study and realized that she had never gotten around to setting up a time to meet with her, but Kara was talking with Hannah afterward and Becca didn't want to interrupt, so she decided she'd call Kara later.

Coffee at Copperchino Friday afternoon wasn't quite the success she'd hoped it would be. With her thoughts so focused on the adventure program, none of the things her friends were talking about—school, work, the movie they saw last week when Becca was up at the camp— seemed all that interesting to her. And the things she wanted to talk about—challenge course initiatives, the relative merits of rival bus companies, and the difficulty of finding qualified ropes course facilitators— clearly weren't of high interest to her friends. She hadn't realized how important shared experiences were; just by separating herself from what the Brios had been doing, she seemed to have separated herself from *them*.

It didn't help that she had to spend the whole weekend trying to get caught up on schoolwork, so she had to turn down Solana's suggestion of a hike in the mountains and Nate's invitation to go paragliding.

"I thought things were supposed to get back to normal once you turned the grant proposal in," Nate said as he walked her to her car.

"They will," Becca promised. "Just as soon as I get caught up at school. I have to put everything else on hold right now. I even told Danny I couldn't go to the camp this weekend—I put him off till next week."

Nate was silent so long that Becca got uncomfortable. "What?" she said. "Are you bugged about Danny?"

Nate shook his head. "No—although you *have* been spending more time with him than with me lately. No, what bothers me is that you're 'putting me on hold.' I didn't think we had the kind of relationship you could just 'put on hold.'"

Becca opened her mouth, but Nate put up a hand to hush her. "Let me finish, okay? I know we agreed to take it slow and not rush things— I'm not talking about changing that. I just don't think you ought to treat people like phone calls. I don't think any *real* relationship should ever be put on hold." He paused a moment, then added seriously, "And that means friends, too."

"The Brios understand!" Becca told him, with no uncertainty

whatsoever. "We made a pact way back in eighth grade to be friends forever. Sure, they've been a little ticked lately, but they'll always be there for me."

"You're lucky to have friends that are totally loyal," Nate said. "But pacts have to work both ways, don't they? If you don't have time for your friends, one of these days you may find out they don't have time for you."

Becca paused. "Are you talking about the Brios, or about you?"

Nate was silent for a long time. Becca felt absolutely sick. *I can't lose Nate*, she cried inside. *But I can't flunk out of my senior year, either. And I can't bail on the adventure program—Ricky and Gina need it so much*. For a minute she felt as if all she wanted to do was get in her car and go far, far away—from homework, deadlines, conflicts, everything. But running away wasn't going to make anything better. *And I'm a make-it-better McKinnon*, she reminded herself. *So how do I make this better?*

"I know things have been really crazy lately," she said at last. "But just let me get through this week and I'll make it up to you—I promise. I'll make sure your birthday party is really special. That's only a week away. Can you just cut me some slack till then?"

Nate looked at Becca a long time. She held her eyes steady on his; she really meant this, and she wanted him to know it. Finally he gave a crooked half-smile. "Okay." He touched her lightly on the cheek then opened her door for her and walked away.

● ● ●

Becca felt a serious case of burnout come on in the following week. She had tons of schoolwork to catch up on, and plenty of work on the adventure program, too, but half the time she found herself flipping on the television or going out to the driveway to shoot hoops "just for a 10-minute break"—that lasted an hour or more. The more her time slipped away, the more desperate she felt, but the more desperate she felt, the harder it seemed to be to force herself to do the work. More than once she would look back over her day and realize that she had wasted several hours that she could have spent with Nate or her friends. Every day she resolved to do better; every day the same thing happened. *What's the matter with me?* she asked over and over. But she didn't know the answer.

The miserable week had one bright spot: On Wednesday she got the good news that her grant proposal had been accepted and she'd be receiving a check by the end of the week! With something of her old enthusiasm, she dialed Nate's number to tell him. To her disappointment, she got the answering machine.

Maybe he's over at Tyler's, she thought, and called there.

"Sorry, Becca," Tyler's mother told her. "Tyler and Nate are out with some of the other guys tonight. I think they were going to see if they could find a game of pickup basketball somewhere. Do you want me to have Ty call you when he gets back?"

"No, that's okay," Becca said. "I'll see him at school tomorrow, I guess."

She started to dial Jacie's number but remembered Jacie was working at Raggs By Razz, so she called Solana instead.

"Sol—the best news! I got the grant!"

"Really?" Solana said. "You mean you're actually calling me and you don't need me to do something for you?"

"That's cold," Becca said. She tried to sound as if she were taking it as a joke, but she had a bad feeling that Solana wasn't teasing.

"That's reality," Solana responded. "I can't remember the last time you called just to talk. But, hey—congratulations on the grant!"

"Thanks," Becca said, but some of the joy had drained out of her.

I'll call Hannah, she decided when she hung up from Solana. *She might be as strong-minded as Solana, but as least she's never as sharp-tongued.* But Hannah wasn't home either.

"She's at the home of a girl named Kara," Hannah's mother told Becca. "You probably know her—I guess Kara's in the Brio Bible study. Hannah is doing one-on-one mentoring with her and is really excited about it. Kara is so eager to hear the gospel!"

"That's great," Becca mumbled, and hung up as quickly as she could. *Kara—and Hannah?* she thought. *With Kara's life history, I'd think Hannah would be the last person she'd want to confide in. Hannah would probably be shocked to hear even half of what Kara's been into. I would be a much better mentor,* she thought resentfully. But honesty forced her to admit that she'd had a chance to mentor Kara and she'd kept putting it off till she was less busy. *I guess Kara couldn't wait forever while I put her on hold.* Becca swallowed hard and went outside to work off her worry shooting hoops.

● ● ●

Danny was waiting for Becca when she drove up to the camp the next Friday after school.

"Have I got a surprise for you!" he said. "Come and see!" He led Becca to the high ropes course and pointed up triumphantly. "We installed a whole new setup. Want to try it out?"

"I don't have a lot of time," Becca said, "but . . . sure, I guess so." She roped up and Danny belayed her while he talked her through the new challenges.

"We call this one the giant trapeze," he said, as Becca climbed to the top of a 40-foot pole. "But I guess maybe you and your Bible-thumping friends might call it 'leap of faith.' It's the ultimate head trip—you'll love it."

"Don't tell me; let me guess," Becca said, balancing on the top of the pole. "I have to leap forward and grab that." She pointed to a trapeze hanging about six feet away. "Okay—here goes nothing!"

Five times she fell, and five times Danny caught her up short with the safety rope. On her sixth try, she caught the trapeze, and the exhilaration she felt as she swung through the air among the vanilla-scented pines seemed to wash away all the stress of the week.

"This is awesome!" she yelled down to Danny. "Got any more like it?"

"How about the giant's swing?" Danny said. "We'll do that one next."

By the time fading light forced them to quit, Becca's enthusiasm for the adventure program matched the height of the tallest ponderosa pine. "I can't wait to get Ricky on the leap of faith," she said, as much to herself as to Danny as they walked back to the camp office. "And Gina—what an opportunity this will give me to talk about taking a real leap of faith and trusting in Jesus!"

Even the tedium of making the necessary corrections and adjustments to the database didn't seem as tiresome as usual, although it took longer because Danny brought supper for both of them from the camp kitchen and then decided to hang around and talk.

"Look, Danny," Becca finally said. "The only reason I came up here is because I'm not paying for camp staff to spend the time inputting this data. But if you're going to sit here anyway, you may as well do the work and let me go home!"

At that Danny laughed and left her alone.

It was completely dark by the time Becca finished and began the slow, careful drive down the twisty mountain road, but she felt lighter inside than she had in a long time. *This adventure course is really going to happen!* she exulted. *I've got the grant; I've got the facility; and the ropes course is going to be exactly what Ricky and Gina need!* She pictured them and the other Community Center kids on the ropes course in their matching adventure program T-shirts, losing their fears and their worries the way she had lost hers today on the ropes.

Note to self, she thought. *Remember to check with Jacie on the T-shirt design.* Once the grant check came through, they'd be able to put the order in.

She pulled into her driveway and noticed Jacie's green Tercel. *Perfect! I can ask her right now!*

Then she noticed that the street was lined with cars—Nate's, Tyler's, and a whole lot more.

Oh no! she gasped. *The party!*

chapter 16

As Becca stood with her hand on the doorknob of her own front door, she felt more apprehensive than she had her first time on the high ropes, her first time paragliding, and at her first basketball tryout, all put together. Part of her wanted to get back in her car and drive until she reached a place where nobody knew her. But no matter how knotted her stomach was and how sweaty her palms were, she knew she had to go in and face her friends—and Nate.

Late. Late. Almost an hour and a half late. If ever Becca wished she were dead, it would be now.

Reluctantly, she pushed open the door. Happy sounds—party sounds—came from the direction of the family room and attached patio, and Becca tried to convince herself that maybe everything was just fine. She didn't really believe it, though, even when she cautiously stepped into the family room and saw a couple dozen guests enjoying themselves there in the family room, on the patio, and in the backyard. Because what she also saw were Solana, Jacie, and Hannah huddled anxiously on the couch and Tyler, Ramón, and Nate standing stiffly apart from the party.

Jacie was the first to see Becca, and she leaped from the couch and ran to Becca, relief and anger mingling in her expression. "We were so worried about you!" she cried. "We called your cell phone, and it rang and rang, and finally Kassy came downstairs and asked us to please quit calling because it was sitting on your bed and the noise was waking Alvaro up."

"We thought you'd had an accident," Hannah accused. "How could you let us worry like that?"

"How . . . could . . . you . . . ditch . . . Nate's . . . party?" Solana spit the individual words out in a low, measured tone that showed clearly that—in her case, anyway—anger was stronger than relief. "Do you have any idea how humiliating it is for him that his girlfriend can't even be bothered to come to his 18th birthday party—at her own house?" She gestured toward the corner where Nate was standing, and unwillingly Becca looked.

Nate had turned to face them, but he hadn't made a move to come to her. He held himself so rigidly that Becca couldn't tell what he was holding in—anger? disappointment? sadness? Tyler's hand was on Nate's shoulder and, in contrast, his expression was perfectly clear: pure anger on his friend's behalf.

"Go talk to him," Jacie hissed, but Becca didn't need to be told. She was already crossing the distance that seemed to be far greater than a simple room-length. As she approached, Nate crossed his arms over his chest—not in the casual, lounging attitude that he so often adopted, but as if he were a fortress and the doors had just been locked shut.

"Nate, I am so sorry," Becca began. "I never meant for this to happen."

Nate looked at her for a long moment. "When you really have time for me," he said finally, "then we'll talk."

● ● ●

Becca didn't think she'd ever spent a longer night. Her sheets tangled around her legs as she twisted one way and the other on her bed, trying to sleep so she could escape her thoughts. Her brain felt like a gerbil running, running, running in its wheel, always running but never getting anywhere. Over and over again Becca relived the evening, trying to think of ways to make things right with Nate. Through her thoughts came a guilty refrain, like the squeak of a gerbil's wheel: *I should have . . . If only . . . Why . . . why . . . why?*

At about five in the morning she finally gave up on sleep and went downstairs. Balloons and streamers and the remains of a broken piñata littered the family room and lawn. *Like my relationships*, Becca thought bitterly. *Trashed*. Wearily, she cleaned up the mess, working quietly so as not to wake up her parents. Right now she didn't want to face anyone. Particularly she didn't want to have to admit to her mom that she had been right. It was too late for that to make a difference anyway.

Carrying an ice bucket of soft drinks from the patio to the refrigerator, Becca noticed the pile of yesterday's mail on the counter. On top, with a Post-It note bearing a smiley face and the note "Congratulations!" in her mother's handwriting (clearly written *before* the party), was an envelope from the grant foundation.

Becca put the soft drinks in the refrigerator, then opened the envelope. There was the check she had worked and waited for so long and so hard—enough to cover insurance, transportation, equipment, and camp fees for an entire year. She tried to feel thrilled, but she just felt tired.

Water running in the upstairs bathroom told her that someone was awake. Feeling as if she needed to be alone to work out her problems, Becca carefully folded the check and put it in her pocket, then took her mother's keys—hers were upstairs in the pockets of the pants she'd worn last night—from the key case by the side door.

I know just where to go, she told herself. *Alyeria!*

chapter 17

When Becca pushed aside a branch to enter Alyeria, she felt as if she were coming home. The clump of aspen trees had been the Brios' secret spot since they found it in elementary school and claimed it as their own imaginary kingdom. As the friends grew up, Alyeria came to represent more than just childhood games; it stood for their friendship and their accountability to one another. Becca half expected to see her friends in the tiny hidden glade inside the clump of trees; they had often gathered there, unplanned, when one of them was having an especially hard time.

But Alyeria was empty now, except for Becca and a cheeky little yellow-rumped warbler hopping along the ground. He announced his claim on the territory to Becca in a buzzy warble, but when she settled down against a fallen log, he flicked his tail in what Becca was sure was an insult and flew off.

Becca flipped open the plastic drinking lid on the 99-cent cup of coffee she'd picked up at the gas station on the way. Generally she preferred hot chocolate to coffee, but after a sleepless night she was desperate for more caffeine than chocolate could give her. She took a tentative sip to make sure it was cool enough to drink, then took a large swallow and began to map out her day.

After she had made a mental list of all the things she needed to accomplish, she waited a little longer in Alyeria, still half hoping that at least one of her friends would come by. Surely if they called her house and learned she'd gone out without telling anyone, they would guess where she was. *But maybe no one called . . .*

By midmorning Becca had to admit to herself that her friends weren't going to come looking for her. *I could call them, but what's the point if they're still mad?* she asked herself. *No—if they're not here for me, they probably don't want to hear what I have to say.* Gloomily, she dumped the last few drops of coffee—long gone cold—onto the ground and left Alyeria.

To distract herself from the gerbil's wheel of guilt that persisted in squeaking in her head, Becca stayed frenetically busy all day. First stop was the savings and loan where her family did their banking. There she endorsed the grant check for some cash and a cashier's check, which she planned to use to open a special account at the bank where the Community Center had its accounts.

Cashing the grant money was a bigger deal than she'd expected. Because of the size of the check and because of Becca's youth, the teller called the manager over to okay the transaction. The manager scrutinized Becca's ID, looked up her account and her parents', examined the letter accompanying the grant check, and even tried to reach the foundation on the phone (which of course no one answered on a Saturday). At last he handed over the money and the cashier's check, but not before giving Becca a little lecture.

"A cashier's check is the same as cash, you know. If you lose it, it's gone."

As if I'm some kind of ignorant kid! Becca fumed. She wanted to tell him, *Listen, Bubba, I wrote the proposal to get that money; don't you think I can be trusted to take care of it?* But she wanted to get out of the bank and on with her business even more, so she held her tongue.

By now she was hungry, plus she didn't want her parents worrying about where she was, so she went home and got something to eat. Mercifully, nobody commented on the party. Nobody had called for her, either.

Becca took her box of adventure program files with her to the bank so that she would have all the information on the Community Center's existing accounts, but when she got to the bank at 12:30 she discovered that it had closed at noon, not at 1:00 as she had thought, so she put the cashier's check in her file box and brought it to the Community Center and locked it in the workroom for safekeeping.

Since her next errand was to buy sleeping bags, Becca got permission to take Gina and Ricky with her to the sporting goods store. The store had a small climbing wall, which fascinated Ricky and Gina, even though they weren't allowed to climb without parental permission, and they talked Becca into taking them to the climbing gear section and showing them all the equipment they'd be using in the adventure program. They looked at sleeping bags and got a good idea of the kind they wanted, but Becca thought she could get a better deal at a cheaper store, so they drove around pricing bags at several stores before making their purchases with the cash from the grant check. They packed as much as they could in the trunk of Becca's car, then crammed the rest in the car.

"Who needs airbags?" Gina laughed, peering over and around sleeping bags on her lap and to either side of her.

By the time they got back to the Community Center, supper was being served in the homeless shelter, so Becca sent Gina and Ricky in to eat and unloaded the car herself. It was satisfying, after all the work she'd done on paper, to actually have something tangible for the adventure program, and she enjoyed the multiple trips it took to carry all the sleeping bags into the workroom, where Mrs. R. had said she could keep them until she found a better storage place. Standing back and admiring the tumbled stacks of sleeping bags, Becca felt, for the first time since the party, that she had done something right. Despite her exhaustion, she went to sign in for her night shift at the shelter with a spring in her step.

● ● ●

After the shelter settled down and was quiet for the night, Becca headed straight for the workroom. Now that she had the grant money, she could finally sign a contract with the bus company, buy an insurance policy, and finalize her agreement with Camp Timberline. And with only two weeks till the launch of the adventure program, she wanted to get everything settled by Monday, if possible, to make sure it was all in effect by the weekend of the trip to camp.

Becca pushed the keyboard aside to make room on the computer desk for her cardboard file box. She pulled out her "transportation" folder (color-coded green, for "go") and flipped through it for the contract from the company she had chosen to use. Wishing she had a cup of hot chocolate to keep her awake, she started reading the fine print.

It felt as if it took forever to understand the contract and fill in the blanks with the necessary information, although when Becca looked at the clock she saw that only half an hour had passed. *I'll put my head down for just a minute,* she thought, stifling a yawn. *After all, I've been up for— what? Twenty-four hours? No—more like 40.* Too tired to worry about the math, Becca laid her head on her arms on the desk.

When she felt herself starting to drool, Becca's head snapped up. *Gotta get these contracts done,* she told herself severely. She pulled out her insurance file, but the language in that contract was even more obscure than in the bus contract, and after a while she realized she'd read three whole pages without comprehending a single sentence.

"Maybe I need some food," she said aloud, breaking the hypnotic hum from the computer. *I was so busy bringing in the sleeping bags that I didn't take time to eat supper,* she realized. *Definitely, food will help me concentrate.*

Quietly she tiptoed from the workroom to the kitchen and opened the refrigerator door to investigate the leftovers from supper. Meatloaf. Her least favorite. Wrinkling her nose, she rummaged around to see what other options she had. As usual, the pickings were slim, unless you counted the industrial-sized cans of pork and beans on the pantry shelves.

"Meatloaf it is," Becca murmured, taking it out of the fridge. At the back of the refrigerator shelf she spied one lone package of soft tortillas. *How would a meatloaf taco taste?* she wondered. *Better than plain meatloaf, anyway. Especially if I fry up the tortillas so they're hot and crispy.* She took out the tortillas, too, and shut the fridge.

Now the kitchen was very dark. Becca looked through the serving window toward the sleeping areas of the shelter. Everyone was quiet. Hoping the light wouldn't wake anyone, she turned on the fluorescent bulb over the stove. Light shone through the serving window, but she didn't think it was bright enough to disturb anyone. Working as quietly as her tired body could, Becca found the smallest frying pan—an iron monster about the size of a birdbath—splashed about an inch of cooking oil in it, and put it on the stove to heat. She had just set about crumbling a slice of meatloaf when the sound of stealthy footsteps caught her attention.

Becca caught up the next-sized frying pan and moved silently to the kitchen door, arm and frying pan raised. Whoever was creeping around would get an ironclad welcome if he didn't belong. With her best action-movie moves, she flung open the kitchen door.

"Yeow! Don't hit me, Becca!" Gina squeaked.

Becca lowered the frying pan and let out her breath. "Gina!" she exclaimed, then quickly lowered her voice to a whisper. "I thought you were a prowler. You sounded so sneaky!"

"I didn't want my mom to know I was up," Gina confessed.

"Why *are* you up?" Becca asked. "Did the light in the kitchen wake you?"

Gina shook her head. "I was awake before that. I was thinking."

Becca waited a bit, then prompted, "Thinking about what?"

"About the adventure program. About today. I had fun."

Becca chuckled. "I've stayed awake some nights thinking about that myself."

"And I was thinking about your friend who was so scared of the ropes course."

"You mean Jacie?"

"Uh-huh. The one who said Jesus carries her in His arms."

"Yeah," Becca said. "I remember that story. I like that story a lot."

"Is it true?" Gina asked. "Is that what Jesus is like? Do you really believe that?"

Becca crouched a little so that her face was level with Gina's. "Yes, Gina, I believe it. I believe it with all my heart. And nothing would make me happier than for you to believe it too."

"If that's what Jesus is like, then I want Him for my friend," Gina said simply. "Only I don't know how to ask Him if He wants to be *my* friend."

"Oh, He wants to be your friend." Becca hadn't known that anyone as tired as she was could feel as happy as she did. "I can help you, Gina. I'll show you how."

She led the younger girl to one of the couches in the shelter day area and helped Gina form her first prayer, asking Jesus to be her Savior and offering her life to Him. Then she wrapped her arms around Gina and Gina hugged her back with all the fierceness Becca had noticed in her the first day they'd met. Only this time the fierceness was directed by love.

"I'm gonna use my diary to write to God like you do, Becca," Gina said after she had wiped away her happy tears. "I haven't written for a long time, but I'm gonna start now."

Becca thought about her journal. How long had it been since she had written a letter to God? How long since she had really prayed, if you didn't count praying with Gina tonight? *I've been so busy, I put God on hold*, Becca realized in dismay. *I'm not the kind of role model Gina thinks I am.*

"Gina," she said, "I think that's a great idea. But I have to tell you something: I haven't done much writing in my journal lately, either. I'm not happy about that, and I'm going to change it. That's something you've made me realize."

"I'm gonna start right now," Gina declared. She gave Becca a stern look. "And I think you better, too."

"I think you're right," Becca said. "Some things are too important to put off." *Like prayer,* she said to herself. *And friends.*

Gina tiptoed into the sleeping area to get her fuzzy purple diary, and Becca dug her journal out of the back of the file box where she'd shoved it weeks ago. Then the two girls sat side by side on the ratty old couch to write their letters to the King on the throne in heaven. When Gina finished, she gave a big sigh and leaned back against the cushions, a look of total contentment on her face.

"Think you can sleep now?" Becca asked.

"I'm gonna go to sleep thinkin' about Jesus like He's my best friend at a sleepover," Gina said. She gave Becca a hug and went back to her mattress on the floor as if she were walking on air.

Becca carried her journal thoughtfully back to the workroom, reflecting on how the letter she had written was mostly confession. *It took Gina to make me see that I've let myself get too busy for You*, she admitted to God. *I thought I was here to help the kids, but like the old cliché, it looks as if they're going to teach me as much as I teach them.*

She put her journal in the file box—in the front, this time—and picked up the insurance contract. As she shifted her tired body on the hard chair, she looked at the piles of sleeping bags. *Maybe I'll read this lying down,* she thought. She unrolled one of the sleeping bags and spread it on the floor. Taking the contract with her, she sank into the downy softness. She read a few paragraphs, then put her head down for just a minute . . .

chapter

Becca jerked awake to a deafening noise.

It's the fire alarm!

She leaped up, scattering the pages of the insurance contract.

Fire! I've got to get the people out of the homeless shelter!

She sped down the short hall to the shelter area, slamming doors as she went. In the shelter sleeping areas, chaos reigned. Someone had pushed back the accordion-pleated divider between the women's section and the men's, and mattresses had been kicked every which way. Children awakened by the alarm were crying—frightened by the noise even if they didn't know what it meant. Randall, one of the mentally ill residents, yelled, "Stop it! Stop it!" and hit himself in the forehead. Becca saw Ricky trying to push his way through the milling bodies to find his mother and little brother. She saw his mouth open in a scream, but she couldn't make out the words over the commotion.

"Quiet!" Becca yelled, but her voice came out in a strangled yelp that couldn't compete with the noise of the alarm and the hubbub of the residents. "Quiet!" she yelled again, mustering all the lung power that made her a tireless runner on the basketball court and the loudest member of the team.

Whether it was her volume, or her air of authority, or sheer providence, the residents were silent for a moment, their attention fixed on Becca. Seizing the opportunity, Becca spoke as commandingly as she could.

"Stay calm; there's no reason to panic." *Oh, yeah?* her gerbil's wheel of worry shrieked. *What about that smoke I'm smelling?* "We're going to leave the building through this door right here." Becca led the way to the door in the northwest corner of the shelter. "We're going to walk, not run, and we're going to do it NOW." She caught Ricky's frightened gaze. "Ricky, I see your mama and your brother. They're fine. You go out now and they'll find you in the parking lot, okay?"

Becca opened the exit door and counted as each person went through. *Twenty-three, twenty-four* . . . With one part of her mind, she was thanking God for Mrs. R.'s insistence that every night shift volunteer note the number of residents at the beginning of each shift. The rest of her concentrated on keeping the residents calm and keeping them moving. *Fire doubles in size every three minutes,* she remembered from Herb's in-service. And she didn't know how long this fire had been burning.

"Thirty-one. Thirty-two." She gave a grateful smile to old Mr. Anderson, who was steering Randall out the door. "You're doing great, Randall—the alarm won't be so loud once you're outside." The smoke was starting to sting her eyes now, and Becca had to fight to keep the panic out of her voice.

"Sixty, sixty-one, sixty-two. That's everybody!" Becca followed the last person out and pushed the door closed on the room that was now swirling with lung-scorching smoke.

Becca took deep breaths of the night air as she tried to think of what to do next. *Find Gordon!* she realized. Her partner on the night shift had been sleeping in the gym when the alarm went off. Where was he now?

The control that had kept her calm enough to evacuate the shelter residents dissolved into near-hysteria as she pictured Gordon trapped in the gym.

"Don't panic," she lectured herself aloud. Gordon was at that in-service too. He would know to go directly out the gym door. *Unless the smoke disoriented him* . . .

But Gordon hadn't gotten disoriented. As Becca looked frantically over the people milling about the dark parking lot, she realized that Gordon was already there, directing them to the far corner of the lot, away from the heat now radiating from the building. "Is everyone out?" he shouted to Becca.

"Yes!" she shouted back. She was about to go help him when the wail of a siren announced the arrival of a fire truck. It jerked to a stop and men jumped off, yanking hoses and axes from the vehicle.

"Thank You, God!" Becca breathed. She ran to the truck just as Herb swung down from the cab.

"What do you have?" he asked Becca.

"The Community Center's on fire!" Becca said. "But everybody's out."

Firemen ran past them toward the building.

"Where did it start?" Herb was brisk and Becca felt an enormous sense of relief knowing she was not in charge any longer.

"I'm not sure," she answered him. "There's so much smoke. I heard the alarm, and I just got everybody out as fast as I could."

Herb nodded. "Good girl." Then he spoke into the two-way radio in his hand. "This is Engine 4. All companies coming in: We have a homeless shelter heavily involved in smoke, all evacuated."

The two firefighters, unrecognizable in their helmets and masks, carried a hose to the gym door. The reflective yellow stripes on their dark jackets glowed as they disappeared through the door. In a moment Becca heard them over Herb's two-way radio. "We're in the gymnasium; we have nothing."

A second fire truck screamed into the parking lot. Over the radio,

Herb directed, "Engine 1, make a hydrant at Main and Sycamore and lay a feeder line to Engine 4."

"We've found fire in the dormitory," came the report from inside.

A ladder truck arrived and Herb radioed, "Truck Company, ventilate the dormitory room." One of the men jumped down from the truck and jogged over to ask where the dormitory room was. Becca pointed to the door that led off the shelter sleeping area.

"What do I do with all my people?" she asked Herb. "They have nowhere to go."

"How many?" Herb asked.

"Sixty-two," Becca answered promptly.

Herb spoke into his radio again. "Dispatcher, I have 62 people here; I need a bus to transport them."

"Where will the bus take them?" Becca asked.

"The fire department doesn't handle that," Herb said. "They can stay in the bus, or someone can call and make arrangements with a motel or some other place."

"I've got to find a phone," Becca said, but Herb put his hand on her arm as she turned to go.

"I need you next to me. If my men get trapped, I'll need someone who can tell me about the inside of the building."

Becca shivered. Until now she had only been worried about the Community Center building and the shelter residents; now she realized that firefighters' lives were at risk. "I'll stay," she told Herb.

"Kitchen is heavily involved in flame," a voice crackled over Herb's radio.

Herb nodded. "That old varnish they used to put on kitchen cupboards goes up like lighter fluid," he explained to Becca.

"Likely source of the fire is from a pan on the lit stove," the voice on the radio reported.

"Oh, no!" Becca clapped her hand over her mouth. Her heart stopped. Tears sprang instantly to her eyes, spilling down her cheeks. "Oh, God," she gasped. "Please. No."

chapter 19

I burned the Community Center down.

Becca could see the sweat on Herb's forehead, could practically smell the heat of the fire. But she felt frozen. Dimly, she was aware of commotion going on around her in the dark—police cars arriving, officers cordoning off the site with barricade tape, news cameras humming. But she seemed to be looking through a window of ice. All she could focus on was the one thought repeating itself over and over: *I did this. This is my fault.*

Two plainclothes men approached Herb. Becca didn't listen as Herb gave them a brief rundown, but then he took her by the arm.

"The fire inspector and the chief incident officer are taking over from me," he said to her. "I'm going to see how those kids are doing before I walk the perimeter of the scene. I thought you'd want to come with me."

Becca nodded, even though she wasn't sure at all that she wanted to face Ricky, Gina, and the others now that she knew the fire was her fault. She trailed a step behind Herb as he led the way to the cluster of residents. When they got close enough to recognize individuals in the yellow circle of the sulphur parking lot light, Gina disengaged herself from her mother's protective embrace and came hurtling to throw her arms around Becca.

Becca pressed her face against the younger girl's hair, inhaling the sharp scent of smoke. The icy shell of shock melted as Gina squeezed her hard, and Becca began to sob.

"Don't cry, Becca." Gina pulled her into the center of the group. "Everybody's okay—look."

Ashamed to meet their eyes, but forcing herself to do it, Becca looked from face to face. Old Mr. Anderson, his long white beard turned sooty with smoke. Ricky, bursting with pride as Herb spoke quietly to him alone. Gina and her mother, looking remarkably alike in their oversized sleep shirts and tousled hair.

"I'm so sorry," Becca said to Gina. "The fire spread to the sleeping area. I don't know whether your things will be all right or not." Her throat felt tight. *They had so little as it was! And now—they may have lost everything!*

"It's okay. I was scared that me and Mom wouldn't get out. Our stuff doesn't matter so much," Gina said.

"But Gina—your diary!" Becca blurted out without thinking.

Gina's mom laid a gentle hand on Becca's arm. "Gina got something a lot more lasting than that diary tonight," she told Becca with a smile that illuminated her tired face and made her look almost as young as Gina. "She got Jesus."

Becca just stood there, trying to comprehend the grace Gina's mom was showing. *Dear Jesus,* she prayed silently, *help me value You as much as this poor woman—no, this rich woman does.* Her reflection was interrupted by a yell from Ricky.

"The bus is comin'," he hollered.

A blue Honda Civic followed the bus and parked neatly beside it. As the bus door opened, so did the Civic door, and out stepped Mrs.

Robeson. Becca's sense of grace was immediately eclipsed by a sense of dread. *I have to face Mrs. R. I have to tell her the fire is my fault.*

Becca thought about hanging back in the crowd of residents, but she knew Mrs. Robeson would look for her first thing for an update. *Besides, I owe it to her to tell her the truth—not make her hear it from the fire inspector.*

Her feet felt like lead as she walked over to Mrs. Robeson, and her heart felt even heavier. But she forced herself to give a concise report of the things she knew Mrs. Robeson needed to know—and the one thing she knew she needed to say.

"Everyone got out safely. The fire spread to the shelter sleeping area, but I don't know where else. We don't know what the damage is yet because the firefighters are still inside." Becca took a deep breath. "The fire started in the kitchen. I think it was because I left a pan of oil on the stove." She braced herself for Mrs. Robeson's response.

"I see." Mrs. Robeson tapped her pen on her ever-present clipboard, then gave Becca a brief nod. "We'll have to talk about that later. Right now our first priority is to get these people settled for the night. I'll need you to help me group them so that families stay together."

Becca nodded. It was like Mrs. R. to deal with the immediate needs of the people rather than to address Becca's carelessness. That would come later. *I wonder whether she'll press charges?* Becca thought. *Is it arson if you set fire to a building by accident?*

Squaring her shoulders, she determined to take responsibility for whatever came. *I've been pushing off my responsibilities for too long,* she realized, remembering how often in the last months she'd left Kassy to pick up her share of chores around the house, and how she'd dumped the work of Nate's party onto the Brios. *Whatever happens next, I'll do my very best with what has to be done right now.*

"Where can we go with everyone tonight?" she asked Mrs. Robeson. "Can the Community Center afford motel rooms for this many?"

"No, we can't," Mrs. Robeson said, "but God's people will meet this need. I will call all the Community Center board members. I'm sure they will be able to make room in their churches for our people until we can make other plans."

"You don't even seem upset," Becca said. She wasn't sure if she was grateful or angry. "You act almost as if this fire doesn't matter."

Mrs. Robeson raised her eyebrows. "Certainly it matters, Becca. But our faith is a faith of hope. We'll look backward to see what we can learn from tonight's tragedy—and yes, I do call it a tragedy. But more important, we'll look forward." She touched the cross that always hung at her neck. "Don't forget, Becca, that our God has a way of turning tragedies into triumph." She tapped her clipboard. "I'll be over there making calls on my cell phone," she said, pointing toward a group of trees away from the crowd.

I wish I could see how that could happen here, Becca thought.

Becca's mom arrived while they were loading the bus. "Honey! I'm so glad you're okay!" she said, wrapping Becca in a hug. "God is so good!"

"I'm glad you're here, Mom," Becca said, and she felt her mother's thin, strong arms tighten around her.

"Your dad and Kassy wanted to come too, but they agreed to stay home with Alvaro. The phone call didn't wake him, thank goodness, so he doesn't know there's been a fire."

Alvaro. Becca hadn't thought about how this fire would impact him. He'd have to know about it, of course; would it bring back the trauma of his own experience when he was caught in his burning house in Guatemala? *Oh, God, my carelessness is going to hurt a lot of innocent people*, Becca prayed. *I'm so sorry.*

Mrs. McKinnon released Becca. "I think someone else is here for you."

Becca turned and found herself nearly smothered by Jacie, Solana, Hannah, and Tyler.

"Kassy called me," Jacie said. "And I called everyone else."

"Oh, Becca," Hannah said. "Is there anything we can do?" She pointed to the station wagon pulling into the parking lot. "That's my mom. She's bringing coffee and hot chocolate and about eight dozen muffins she pulled out of the freezer."

"Think we could serve the people on the bus before they leave?" Solana asked. "I bet they've been out here in the cold a long time."

"I always knew Becca would get you to volunteer at the Community Center one way or another," Tyler teased Solana. "I just didn't think she'd have to burn the place down to do it."

"Tyler!" Jacie scolded. "Show a little sensitivity! You make it sound like the fire is Becca's fault!" She dragged him off to help Hannah's mom unload the goodies.

If you only knew, Becca thought.

As Hannah and Solana followed Jacie and Tyler to the station wagon, another figure caught Becca's eye. Tall and long-limbed, he was only a silhouette as he walked slowly across the dark parking lot, but Becca would recognize him anywhere.

Nate.

He stopped a few feet away from Becca and stood looking at her as if he didn't know what to say. Becca had a dozen things she *wanted* to say, but she didn't trust her voice to utter any of them without breaking.

Nate opened his arms and Becca moved into them.

chapter 20

On Sunday morning, Becca dragged herself downstairs in time to go to church with the rest of the family.

"Go back to sleep if you want," Mr. McKinnon said. "You can miss church for once."

"No," Becca mumbled, weariness blurring her speech. "I'm not putting God on hold any more."

"Catching up on your sleep doesn't mean you're putting God on hold, Honey," Becca's mom said gently.

"I want to go to church, Mom," Becca insisted. "I *need* to go."

Although the fire had happened too late on Saturday night to make the Sunday morning paper, Becca's whole church knew about it by the end of the service. First off, the pastor welcomed "our guests from Outreach Community Center"—the homeless shelter residents who had spent the night in the church fellowship hall. Then he described Becca's role in evacuating the shelter and asked the congregation to give thanks for lives spared and to pray for a solution to the Community Center's and the shelter residents' immediate needs.

"I believe God makes us aware of a need so He can use us to meet that need," he concluded. "How can you help? Through prayer? With your money? By providing meals, bedding, clothing for the residents who will be staying at our church temporarily?"

After the service, Becca was overwhelmed by the number of people who came to talk with her and with the shelter residents.

"I felt a whole new spirit in church today, didn't you?" Becca's mom said on the way home from church. "Our congregation has always supported the Community Center financially, but I think today they saw the human side of it for the first time."

"And smelled it," said Kassy. "Those homeless people reeked of smoke." Becca was about to snap at Kassy when she continued. "All they have are the clothes they were wearing in the fire—can you imagine? I've got some jeans and cute tops that I bet would fit Becca's friend Gina. Would it be okay if I gave them to her, Mom?"

"More than okay, Kassy." Mrs. McKinnon smiled. "That would be wonderful."

● ● ●

Sunday afternoon, Becca drove to the Community Center. She would rather have stayed away, but the fire inspector had asked to meet with her and Mrs. Robeson at the site.

Yellow "fire scene" barricade tape fluttered warnings around the northwest corner of the building, where most of the fire damage seemed to be. But the main entrance of the Community Center, on the east side, was open, and Becca let herself in.

The smell of smoke in the lobby was so strong that Becca thought the fire wasn't out. She stepped back, ready to run out the door, when she saw Mrs. Robeson and the fire inspector.

"The smoke smell—is that okay?" Becca asked.

The inspector nodded. "It will take a lot of scrubbing, painting, and new carpets before the smell is gone. Smoke does as much damage as fire—sometimes more."

"Oh." Becca bit her lip. *One more thing to feel guilty about.*

Mrs. Robeson gestured to the chairs in the lobby. "The fire inspector wants to ask you some more questions about last night, Becca," she said.

Becca sat down. She wondered why they were meeting here in the lobby instead of in Mrs. R.'s office, but she figured she was there to answer questions, not to ask them.

"I understand that you claimed responsibility last night for starting the fire," the inspector began. Then he began a series of questions about why she was in the kitchen, what she had been doing before, what exactly she did with the stove, and on and on. When Becca thought she had answered every possible question, he started over, asking the same questions in a slightly different way. *What is he trying to find out?* Becca asked herself. *I've told him everything I know.* Just when she felt she couldn't stand the interrogation any longer, the inspector turned to Mrs. Robeson.

"She hasn't contradicted herself once," he told Mrs. Robeson. "I'm confident her statement is the truth. The fire was an accident; she didn't set it intentionally."

"Of course she didn't set it intentionally," Mrs. Robeson said sharply. "Is that what you were trying to determine? I could have told you that without you trying to trip the poor girl up."

"I take it then that you will accept the verdict of accident and not press charges?"

"Pressing charges was never under consideration," Mrs. Robeson said. "Since you don't know Becca, I can't expect you to believe that she would never intentionally do anything to harm the Center, but surely you can agree that she wouldn't set a fire that would destroy the equipment for her own adventure program."

"What did you say?" Becca felt cold all over.

"I'm sorry, Becca. The fire gutted the kitchen, the homeless shelter, and the workroom where your sleeping bags were," Mrs. Robeson said. "My office didn't burn entirely, but it's badly smoke-damaged."

"No!" Becca jumped to her feet. "No! I can't believe it. Can I see?"

At the inspector's nod, Becca raced across the lobby and down the hall. There debris slowed her down, and she picked her way cautiously to the workroom. When she looked in the door, she felt as if she'd had the wind knocked out of her. Everything was black. The storage shelves—finished with the same varnish Herb said was so flammable—were bubbled as if they were coated with cooled lava. Everything that had been on the shelves—reams of paper for the copy machine, the stacks and stacks of used paper for recycling—had been reduced to unrecognizable piles of ash. Closing her eyes, Becca could picture how all that paper would blaze. The brand-new sleeping bags were destroyed. Her file box, gone.

Becca began to shake uncontrollably. Tears were running down her cheeks when Mrs. Robeson came up behind her.

"I know it's a loss, Becca," she said. "But perhaps you can replace the sleeping bags."

"It's not just the sleeping bags," Becca wailed. "The cashier's check—almost the entire amount of the grant—was in my file box. And now it's gone!"

● ● ●

"I'm sorry, Mrs. R.," Becca said, after the fire inspector had left and they were sitting together in the lobby. "I really let you down. With the fire, and with the adventure program, too. I . . . I don't know what to say."

"'Sorry' is a good start," Mrs. Robeson said. "But your letting me down is not what concerns me. There are much bigger consequences to your actions than that, Becca."

"I know," Becca said miserably. "I was trying to make things better, and instead I've ruined everything."

"Oh, you aren't that important," Mrs. Robeson said crisply. "Don't think that all by yourself you're going to ruin a ministry that belongs to God. Your carelessness was horribly destructive—but God's power is tremendously creative. I don't think for a minute that we've seen the last of what God plans to do here at Outreach Community Center."

Becca looked at Mrs. Robeson in awe. *She really means that!* Humbly, Becca said, "Will you let me help? I know I can never make up for what I did, but whatever you tell me to do, I'll do." A terrible thought struck her. "Unless, of course, you don't want me around at all."

"I honestly haven't decided what to do about you yet," Mrs. Robeson said soberly. "Under normal circumstances, I would take away your responsibility for the night shift at the very least. But as we don't have a night shift currently, that's hardly relevant." She shook her head. "I'll need some time to think this through, Becca. You disregarded our kitchen policies about never leaving open flame unattended, but from what the residents tell me, you also did an outstanding job evacuating the building. And certainly you've already received consequences for your carelessness."

Becca nodded. *My dream of an adventure program—up in flames, literally.*

"Excuse me a moment, Becca," Mrs. Robeson said, rising and moving to the lobby door. "Perhaps this man is someone else from the fire department." Opening the door, she said, "The Community Center is temporarily closed. Perhaps I can help you?"

"Hope so," the visitor said. "I'm looking for a gutsy kid named Becca."

Becca looked at the man standing outside the plate glass door.

"Otis!"

chapter 21

"What are you doing here?" Becca cried, rushing to fling her arms around Otis. "I've been so worried about you! I didn't think I'd ever see you again! Are you all right?"

"Same old Becca," Otis noted in a satisfied voice. "Always got plenty to say. I saw the fire on the news today. I remembered you always talked about the Community Center—I even called here for you one time."

"I know!" Becca said. "I got your message, but I didn't know how to reach you. Where have you been?"

"One question at a time, Kid," Otis said with a grin. "I'm still working on 'what are you doing here?' So anyway, I perked up when they said the fire was at the Community Center, and then when I saw you on the TV, I figured I'd better get over here and see what I can do to help."

"I was on TV?" Becca said.

"Sure. Haven't you been watching the news?"

Becca shook her head. "My little brother got burned in a fire and we don't want him seeing this one on TV."

"Makes sense," Otis said. "Anyway, like I said, anything I can do, you just let me know. I can't do any heavy lifting since the accident, but I'm still on disability so I've got plenty of time." He nodded politely to Mrs. Robeson. "If you're in charge here, ma'am, then I guess I'm making this offer to you."

"I'm the director," Mrs. Robeson replied, "and I thank you—sir."

"You're on disability?" Becca burst in. "And you can't do heavy lifting? What happened when you fell? I heard you were in rehab but I never knew where."

Otis laughed. "Guess we got some catching up to do, Kid. If you're done here," he looked inquiringly at Mrs. Robeson, "what do you say we go for coffee somewhere?"

"Go ahead, Becca," Mrs. Robeson said. "We'll talk again later."

● ● ●

"So, Kid," Otis said when they were settled in a vinyl booth at Mimi's Café with two large slices of apple pie in front of them, "looks like you had a pretty rough night of it last night."

"Oh, Otis! It's so awful, you can't imagine!" Suddenly all Becca's questions faded to the back of her mind; all she wanted to do was to pour out the whole sorry story. "I had such big dreams . . ." She explained about Ricky and Gina, and her hopes for what an adventure program could do for them. Otis listened attentively, and she could see him getting caught up in her excitement over the high ropes course, and beaming with pride for her when she told him about winning the grant.

She told him about her failures, too—not just the fire, but about putting Nate, her friends, her family, and even God on hold. "And all the money for the adventure program went up in smoke in the fire," she concluded, "so there won't be any adventure program."

"Why not?"

Becca quit fiddling with her straw and looked up at Otis. He looked as if he really wanted to know—could it be that he hadn't been listening?

"I'm serious, Kid," Otis said. "You've convinced me how important this adventure program is. You can't just give up on it now."

"Yeah, right," Becca said. She was starting to feel a little annoyed. Didn't he think she'd gone over the possibilities in her mind a hundred times already?

"Hmm. I see it's my turn to talk for a while," Otis said. "You wanted to know what happened after I crashed, right? Well, I woke up in the university hospital with casts from my neck to my toes and pins in parts of my body I didn't know could *be* pinned. I lay like that for longer than I care to remember." He grimaced at the memory. "When they finally sawed those casts off, I was left with the puniest, palest-looking body you'd ever want to see. My skin looked like something that'd been living under a rock."

"You look good now," Becca said. She meant it. He *was* paler than she remembered him, and thinner, too, but she'd never call him puny. "How'd you do it?"

Otis pointed a finger at her. "*Now* you're asking the right questions. How I did it is this: The PT—that's 'physical therapist'—told me I had two choices. I could accept that my body was beat up pretty bad and learn to get along in a wheelchair, or I could make up my mind to fight like mad to get stronger. He gave me a quote to think about: 'Whatever doesn't kill me makes me stronger.'"

Becca twisted her mouth into an ironic smile. "I have a quote like that. 'I can do all things through Christ who gives me strength.'"

"*That's* the kind of thing I had to think about," Otis said. "And believe me, I had plenty of time to think. I asked myself, am I going to lie down and give up? Or am I going to grab hold and dig in and keep looking till I find some core of strength? Well, you can guess what I chose. And I can tell you, Kid, I'm living proof that sometimes the very best things come out of what you think is the very worst." He put his elbows on the table and leaned toward Becca. "So I'm telling you: You got two choices. What's it going to be? Give up or grab hold?"

This was a side of Otis that Becca had never seen. He seemed so intense, so convinced. She couldn't bring herself to say she was giving up, but she wasn't going to lie to Otis, either. She tried to explain it to him. "Otis, I have no money."

"You started with no money, right?"

"Well . . . right, but it took forever to get everything together for the grant proposal, and all that paperwork was in the files that burned. And besides, I could never get another grant in time. I still have to cancel our trip for the end of October."

"What would it cost just to do that trip?"

Becca had gone over the budget numbers so many times that she could rattle off exactly what it would cost to rent the camp for a weekend, to hire a bus, and so on. Otis wrote the numbers on a paper napkin and added them up.

"Plus I'd need insurance," Becca said, and quoted him the cost for a year.

"Bet you don't have to pay that all at once, though," Otis said. "I'll put down the cost of a quarterly payment." He added it to the subtotal and pushed the napkin over to Becca. After the numbers she'd been working with for a full-year program, it didn't look so daunting.

"But it's not just money," Becca said, to herself as much as to Otis. "There's facilitators. You don't know how hard it is to find good ropes course facilitators."

"How many would you need—just to get started?" Otis asked. "Just for this first trip in October."

"Well, I guess really just one," Becca admitted. "Especially if the other volunteers were there to help kids get into their harnesses and stuff."

"Hey, Kid, you're looking at a high ropes facilitator right here." Otis tapped himself on the chest. "Fully certified and at your service. No charge."

"You're kidding," Becca said.

Otis shook his head.

"Wow, Otis, that's incredible. Thanks! Only . . ." Becca hesitated. She didn't want to hurt Otis's feelings, and she didn't want to turn down what might be a solution to one of her problems, but . . . *God, You know I committed to having only Christian facilitators. Should I give up on that?* Becca didn't get any audible answers to her quick prayer, but she knew that if she gave in on this she'd be on the road to putting God's priorities on hold for her own.

"I really appreciate the offer, Otis, but I made a commitment to staff the whole program only with Christians. Nothing personal." Inside she cringed, wondering how Otis would respond.

He laughed out loud. "For a smart kid, you haven't really been getting what I've been saying, have you?"

Becca was mystified. "Uh—I guess not."

"I even left a message that I met your friend."

Becca just looked blankly at him.

"Jesus," Otis said. "I met your friend *Jesus*. Through a chaplain in the hospital who just wouldn't give up on me. Kind of reminded me of you—not a quitter, you know?" He gave Becca a sly smile.

"You met Jesus? You mean—you're a Christian?" Becca felt herself get all goose-bumpy.

"Jesus is who I grabbed hold of to find the strength to get me through rehab. I can do all things through Christ who gives me strength, you know."

"Otis, are *you* quoting Scripture to *me?*" Becca said.

"Somebody has to," Otis replied. "You seem to have forgotten it's true."

Becca thought of the picture on her bulletin board and all the months of praying for Otis. And now here he was—teaching her about how God works. "You're right, Otis. I guess I did forget. But it is true."

"Darn right," Otis said. "And if God can save somebody like me, He's not going to have problems doing what He wants with your adventure program."

J O U R N A L

Wednesday, Oct. 15
Dear God,

   You are amazing. more than amazing. You're so . . . oh, I don't even have the words to say how awesome you are.

Becca stopped writing in her journal—a new one, the twin of the one she had just given to Gina—and closed her eyes. Just thinking about God overwhelmed her sometimes. She didn't remember ever having that experience before. *Maybe Otis was right—whatever doesn't kill me makes me stronger. Or at least makes my faith stronger.* She turned back to her journal.

   If I listed all the amazing things you've done lately, I'd have this journal filled in no time. Keeping everybody safe in

THE FIRE. BRINGING OTIS TO YOU. BRINGING GINA TO YOU. OPENING UP ALL THOSE CHURCHES TO THE SHELTER RESIDENTS. LETTING ME MEET OTIS AGAIN.

AND MY FRIENDS. DEAR GOD, THANK YOU FOR MY FRIENDS. THANK YOU FOR MAKING ME BRAVE ENOUGH TO APOLOGIZE FOR THE WAY I TOOK THEM FOR GRANTED. THANK YOU FOR THE WAY THEY LOVE ME ANYWAY. SOMETIMES I THINK THAT'S AS AMAZING AS ANYTHING YOU'VE DONE!

I DON'T REALLY KNOW IF I CAN DO ALL THINGS, GOD, EVEN WITH CHRIST TO GIVE ME STRENGTH, BUT I DO KNOW THAT YOU CAN. SO I'M JUST GOING TO DO THE BEST I CAN, WITHOUT PUTTING MY FRIENDS OR MY FAMILY OR MY SCHOOLWORK ON HOLD ANYMORE. AND IF YOU WANT THINGS TO HAPPEN WITH THE ADVENTURE PROGRAM, LIKE OTIS SEEMS TO THINK YOU DO—WELL, I'M JUST GOING TO TRUST YOU TO MAKE THEM HAPPEN.

IF THAT'S NOT THE WAY YOU WANT IT, PLEASE LET ME KNOW SOMEHOW.

YOURS FOREVER,
BECCA

Becca closed her journal and galloped downstairs to the kitchen. "I'm starving! Is supper ready yet?"

Her mom held up a hand to quiet her and spoke into the phone. "But what prompted this?" She grabbed the newspaper from the counter and began flipping through it. "No, I didn't read the paper this morning. Where did you say the article was?" She held up the page to show Becca. There, in a full-color photo, looking stubborn and yet somehow charming, were Ricky and Gina.

"Can I see this?" Becca asked, taking it from her mom without waiting for permission. Mrs. McKinnon quickly finished her conversation and put down the phone.

"Yes!" her mom cried, pumping her fist in the air and then breaking into what Becca could only imagine were disco moves from the '70s. Frankly, they were kind of scary, but Becca guessed they meant her mom was really happy.

"Hallelujah!" Mrs. McKinnon shouted, which Becca found equally scary coming from her generally reserved mother. She started to wonder whether she should find her dad or call a doctor.

"The zoning board changed their decision!" Mrs. McKinnon grabbed Becca's hands and danced her around the kitchen table. "They're going to let us expand the homeless shelter when we rebuild!"

"Yes!" shouted Becca. "Hallelujah!"

"Are you okay in there?" came her father's voice from the kitchen doorway. Behind him were Kassy and Alvaro. Kassy looked concerned, but Alvaro just looked like he wanted to join the party.

"Yes!" he cried, slipping past his dad and joining Becca and her mom in their jig around the table. "Si! Si! A! B! C!"

Becca and her mom collapsed, laughing, into chairs at the table and motioned for Kassy and Mr. McKinnon to join them.

"The zoning board okayed the homeless shelter expansion," Mrs. McKinnon explained. "I guess it was because of this article." She took the newspaper and began skimming. "It's a follow-up story on the Center fire. It looks like the reporter interviewed some of the shelter clients for human interest." She read a little more, then chuckled. "He says most of the adults were shy about going on the record but not 'two outspoken youngsters named Ricky and Gina'! I get the impression they rather captivated him."

Becca scooted her chair over so she could read the article too.

"Listen to this! Gina told the reporter that she's writing letters to God asking for a 'bigger and better' shelter!"

"Bless the child," Mr. McKinnon said, with a catch in his voice. He pulled Alvaro up onto his lap.

"Oh—they interviewed Mrs. Robeson, too!" Becca said.

"Let me see." Mrs. McKinnon pulled the paper back in front of her. "She says that the Community Center has long needed a larger shelter facility, but that the zoning board, 'in their infinite wisdom,' has consistently ruled against it."

Mr. McKinnon gave a loud belly-laugh. "I'll bet the zoning board saw that article and knew they'd hear it from their constituents, and that's why they changed their decision so fast." He leaned over to look at the photo of Ricky and Gina. "Those two little characters have a bigger influence than they know."

"Oh, listen, Becca!" Mrs. McKinnon exclaimed. "Ricky and Gina told the reporter all about the adventure program, too, and how the sleeping bags and the funds were destroyed in the fire. Oh! And the reporter is inviting the community to rally with funds for rebuilding the homeless shelter *and* for the adventure program!"

"Yes!" said Kassy. Then, as everyone looked at her, *"What?"*

A loud knock sounded at the side door and before anyone could answer it, Jacie, Hannah, and Solana burst in.

"Sol read the paper and called us," Jacie explained breathlessly. "Isn't it terrific? You'll have the money for the adventure program after all!"

"It's only a week and a half till the first trip," Becca reminded her. "The money's going to have to come in pretty fast."

"What—and you think that's too hard for God?" Hannah said. "This is the God that took care of everybody the night of the fire, remember?"

"Yeah—come on, Becca," Solana said. Jacie and Hannah stared at her, and she added, "Not that I believe it—but then, a lot of things have happened lately that I would never have believed."

●●●

And the money did come in. From the churches who were housing the displaced homeless shelter residents, from local businesses, from individuals. Children's Sunday school classes gave nickels and dimes and quarters. The members of the Brio Bible study committed to skipping lunch every Thursday and giving their lunch money toward restocking the homeless shelter pantry. Contractors volunteered their services toward rebuilding the Community Center, and a local architect offered to draw up plans for the expansion for free. So many offers of help came over the phone that Angela was swamped, so Otis set himself up next to her at the receptionist's desk to take calls.

"I'll tell you, Honey," Angela confided to Becca, "that friend of yours is some smooth-talker. He's got red-hot conviction. He gets those donors on the line, and by the time they hang up, they're so on fire for this project that they've gone and pledged twice as much as they planned! And they're glad to do it, too!"

On the Wednesday before the weekend Becca had hoped would be the launch of the adventure program, Otis called her at home after school. "Get yourself to the Community Center, Kid—I've got a surprise for you."

Becca strapped Alvaro in his car safety seat—it was her day to watch him—and drove right over. Clustered behind the receptionist's desk, beside Otis and Angela, were Jacie, Solana, Hannah, Tyler, and Nate. All of them were wearing green T-shirts with Jacie's logo for the adventure program. Alvaro ran up to Jacie, and she slipped a size XS over his head.

"You had the T-shirts made!" Becca said. "That is a cool surprise! Now I just hope we get to use them sometime."

"The surprise isn't over yet, Kid," Otis said. "I hope you haven't made any plans for the weekend." He nodded at Nate and Tyler, who ducked down for something they had apparently hidden behind the desk. After a few moments of scuffling noises, they dragged a tarp out from behind the desk. The tarp was loaded with sleeping bags.

"How did you get these?" Becca shrieked. She stooped to examine them. They were even better quality than the bags destroyed in the fire.

"Fabyan Sporting Goods donated them," Otis said. "I don't think it hurt that I promised 'em a poster for their store window with a picture of Ricky and Gina announcing that Fabyan's is a proud sponsor of the Outreach Adventure Program. After that newspaper article, helping those kids is good for business."

Next Solana reached under the receptionist counter. She handed Becca a five-pound coffee can filled with coins and bills. "From the fire station," she said. "Herb and the rest of the company from Engine 4 took up a collection for the kids. He called the Center and Otis told him how much it would cost to make the quarterly payment on an insurance policy, and they raised that amount. Herb said," Solana quoted sassily, "that he thinks you're going to need insurance."

Hannah stepped forward and handed Becca an envelope. Becca tore it open and found a completed contract from the bus company—donating the services of a bus and driver for the coming weekend.

"The owner of the bus company goes to my church," Hannah explained. "He has five children—three adopted at older ages—and he said he wanted to do this to help the Center kids."

Becca shook her head. "This is unbelievable!" She looked at the date on the contract. "I don't want to seem ungrateful, but do you think he'd let us use the bus a different weekend if we can't come up with the money for this weekend?"

"Slow learner, sometimes, isn't she?" Otis said to the others. "Go ahead, Jacie; guess we better not keep her in suspense."

All Jacie gave Becca was a slip of paper with a number on it. "The confirmation number for your reservation at Camp Timberline this weekend," she said. "No charge. Turns out they didn't have any paying customers wanting to use the camp this weekend, so they said the adventure camp can come for free, if you'll sign a contract that you'll use them the next time you need a camp."

All at once, Becca felt as if her legs wouldn't hold her anymore. She sat right down on the floor. Clutching one of the sleeping bags to her, she looked from one friend to another, her cheeks hurting with the size of her smile.

"Where's your camera, Hannah?" Tyler said. "We may never see this again—Becca speechless!"

chapter 23

Becca ran her hand over the slippery nylon casing of a sleeping bag and jingled the can of coins—tangible proof that the adventure program would go on after all. But she knew, even if her friends didn't, that it wasn't a sure thing that she would be part of it. That depended on what Mrs. Robeson decided.

With a quick explanation to her friends, Becca went to find Mrs. R. in her temporary office in a corner of the multipurpose room. Alvaro stayed in the lobby, building a fort out of sleeping bags with Nate and Tyler.

Mrs. Robeson looked up from the card table she was using as a desk and invited Becca to sit in a folding chair. "Otis has been keeping me up-to-date on the support that's coming in for the adventure program," she said. "I understand you have enough resources now to launch it this weekend as you originally planned. Is that a possibility, or are there other obstacles Otis is not aware of?"

"It's completely possible," Becca said. "I would need to get medical releases signed for all the kids because my copies burned, but otherwise everything is in order. Except . . ."

Mrs. Robeson waited.

"Except I'm not sure of my status as a Community Center volunteer," Becca finished. She decided to be blunt. "Do you trust me to launch this program, or shall I try to find someone else to do it?"

"Would you do that, Becca? Could you hand the program over to someone else to run?"

Becca's heart sank. So that's what Mrs. R. had decided. "Yes," she said slowly. "If I have to, that's what I'll do." *At least the kids will get to go,* she told herself. She tried not to imagine what the weekend would be like, sitting home while the Brios and the kids were up at Camp Timberline.

"Can the program succeed without you?" Mrs. Robeson asked.

"Yes!" Becca assured her. "Yes, I know it can! I don't have to be there for it to work." Her heart pounded. Would Mrs. R. pull the whole program just because Becca couldn't be there to run it?

"Then I think you've learned a lot, Becca," Mrs. Robeson said. "You no longer seem to suffer from the delusion that God's work cannot proceed without you." She smiled. "That's a sign of maturity." She opened a file folder on her desk. "Now, to answer your question: Yes, I do trust you to launch the adventure program. I've thought and prayed about this, and I've decided to give you a second chance—not just with the adventure program, but as a night-shift volunteer for the homeless shelter, as well."

Becca's breath caught in her throat. After thinking she was out of the adventure program, to realize she was back in—it was the best news yet.

"Our God is a God of second chances," Mrs. Robeson said, as if she sensed Becca's amazement. "It's only right that we should offer them too."

"Thank you, Mrs. R.!" Becca finally managed to sputter. "Thank you!"

Mrs. Robeson acknowledged Becca's thanks with a nod, then consulted her file. "Our host churches are supplying all our staffing needs for our homeless clients right now, and I am hopeful that many of these volunteers will continue even after the clients have moved out of the churches and into our rebuilt shelter. But I would be happy to have you as part of our volunteer core."

"Thank you," Becca said again. "Do you need to know right now? I think I'd like to ask my parents what they think."

"That might be wise," Mrs. Robeson said calmly. "I'll plan on you for the adventure program then, and wait to hear from you about the homeless shelter night shift." She stood, and Becca knew the interview was over.

"Hallelujah! Yes! Yes! Yes!" she yelled as she raced back to the lobby. She grabbed Nate by the hand and danced around the sleeping bag fort. "We're going to Camp Timberline! The adventure program is a reality!"

● ● ●

WeDNesDay, oct. 22
Dear GOD,
    YOU'Ve DONe More THaN I ever ImaGINeD.
I caN HarDLY BeLIeVe THaT we Have
everYTHING we NeeD TO Take THe KIDS TO
caMP THIS weekeND. aND YOU MaDe IT aLL
HaPPeN. WHICH reMINDS Me—I'M reaLLY GOING
TO TrY TO STOP caLLING IT "MY" aDVeNTUre
ProGraM aND STarT caLLING IT YOUr
aDVeNTUre ProGraM.
    NOW aBOUT YOUr HOMeLeSS SHeLTer. I
reaLLY WaNT TO HeLP, aND I reaLLY LOVe
BeING WITH THe PeOPLe. BUT I aLSO WaNT TO

STICK WITH THE aDVenTure Program, aT LeasT unTiL iT's reaLLY uP anD runninG, anD WiTH THe Brio BiBLe STUDY. anD i Don'T wanT To BLOW OFF mY FrienDS anD FamiLY any more. i've Been THinkinG aBouT WHaT mom anD DaD aSkeD me. i THouGHT THeY'D TeLL me WHaT To DO, BuT inSTeaD THeY aSKeD me WHaT i THouGHT Your Priorities Were For me. TeLL me iF i'm wronG, GOD, BuT i THink You neeD me To Learn To SaY no SomeTimes. i'LL keeP PrayinG aBOUT iT, BuT iF You Don'T SHOW me anYTHinG DiFFerenT, i'm GoinG To TeLL mrs. roBeSOn THaT i won'T Be DoinG THe niGHT SHiFT anYmore.

> Yours Forever,
> BeCCa

Becca closed her journal and looked at the clock. "Hey, Alvaro," she called, walking down the hall to his room. "Want me to read you *The Cat in the Hat Comes Back* before I tuck you in?"

● ● ●

"How cool is this?" Tyler said. He and Nate were pulling duffels and sleeping bags out of the cargo compartment of the rented bus and heaving them onto growing piles of luggage. "All these kids here for the adventure program—and at least half of them aren't Christians yet."

"That could change for some of them this weekend," Hannah said. She looked through her camera to frame a shot, but didn't take one. "Not enough light."

"Time for me to do my stuff," Solana said.

"Does Ramón know about this?" Hannah asked. "I don't like it."

"Yes, he knows," Solana said, exasperated. "He thought it was funny." She narrowed her eyes. "You think he shouldn't trust me?"

"Oh, no!" Hannah said. "I just think it's mean to—"

"There he is," Becca whispered, pointing to a figure loping down the trail from the lodge.

"He's not going to know what hit him," Solana said. She looked at Hannah. "Don't worry. I'm not going to flirt. I'm just going to keep him occupied. I want Becca to keep her commitment to have only Christians staffing this camp, and you know that doesn't describe me."

"Yet," murmured Hannah.

"So I'm really glad I can help out by keeping Danny out of the way," Solana continued, ignoring Hannah. "Now excuse me while I go head him off at the 'pass,' so to speak." And with an exaggerated swing of the hips, she headed up the trail.

Saturday's ropes course challenge was all that Becca hoped it would be. Otis turned out to be a terrific facilitator. He came up with the idea of pairing each kid from the Community Center with one of the Brio friends for a challenge he called "the Tarzan walk." Becca watched with delight as Nate led Ricky out onto the cable and showed him how to hold the dangling "vines"—actually ropes suspended from a higher cable—to get his balance. But the vines were spaced so far apart that Ricky had to let go and hold on to Nate's arm, relying on Nate's experience and balance to keep them both on the cable. Ricky was thrilled when he managed to cross the entire distance without falling.

But the best part came that night, in front of the fireplace, when Otis shared a little of his own life.

"I want you to think about that cable as a symbol for your life," he told the kids. "Used to be I thought I could walk it just fine on my own. And you know what? For a long time that's what I did. Need somebody's help? Not me! That stuff was for weaklings."

Becca noticed some of the more street-smart kids nodding.

"Now—any of you want to call me a weakling?" Otis looked around the room as all the kids shook their heads.

"No way!" Guillermo said. "You the man!" He had been following

Otis around ever since Otis had raced across the Burma bridge—blindfolded.

"Got that right," Otis confirmed. "And you know what? Comes a day when even 'the man' gonna fall off that cable. One day it happened to me."

He told the kids about his paragliding accident, and how he'd discovered that only Jesus gave him the strength he needed for recovery.

"One of these days, you're gonna need someone stronger than you," he said to Guillermo. "And so are you, and you, and you." The kids listened wide-eyed as Otis pointed to them. "You remember how it was on the Tarzan walk?" he said to Ricky. "What would've happened to you without Nate?"

"I be fallin' all the time."

"That's right." Otis nodded. "And without Jesus holding on to me on my cable—my life—*I* be falling all the time. That's why I let Him be my leader. All the time." He paused, then added, "You want to hear about it, you come talk to me. Or talk to Becca or Nate or one of the other leaders."

● ● ●

After the kids were asleep in their cabins, the friends gathered in the lodge to talk over the day. Solana had somehow managed to convince Danny that he ought to walk "bulldog"—patrol around the cabins to keep order in case anyone woke up.

After all their excited stories about their time with the kids had dwindled to a contented silence, Becca cleared her throat.

"I have an announcement to make," she said. "Otis and I have been talking, and if it's okay with Mrs. R., he's agreed to take over leadership of the adventure program. I just don't have the time it deserves," she admitted, "and he'll be able to keep it going even after we all go off to college next fall."

Becca could tell from their faces and the brief silence that her friends were surprised, but then they burst into a babble of enthusiasm.

"You'll be great, Otis!" Tyler said. "Count me in whenever you need a volunteer, will you?"

"Plan on a winter camp in January, then," Otis told him. "I hope all of you will be there."

"Does this mean no more going crazy?" Nate said quietly to Becca. "Maybe you'll even have a life again?"

Becca curled her fingers between his. "No more going crazy. I promise."

Just then Danny stuck his head in the door. "Solana, I thought you were going to walk bulldog with me," he complained.

"Not tonight, Danny."

"Oh, Becca," he added as an afterthought, "I almost forgot. The camp director left this message for you." He handed Becca a slip of paper and let Solana steer him back out the door.

"Hmm . . . so it's 'Becca' now, not 'Brown Eyes'?" Tyler said. "Looks like Solana's doing her job well. Maybe a little too well?"

"It has its hazards," Solana admitted. "I'm just glad we're here only for a weekend, not a week. Next time I'm bringing Ramón. He'll keep Danny occupied."

"What's the message from the camp director?" Jacie asked. "I hope he's not upset with anything we're doing."

Becca shook her head. "Just the opposite. He says he's really impressed with what he's seen today—and all along the way as I was developing the adventure program. He had to approve all the plans," she added in explanation.

"So he sent you a note to compliment you?" Jacie said. "That's sweet."

"Not just to compliment me," Becca said, rereading the message. "He wants to talk with me before we leave tomorrow—about taking a part-time job here."

"A job? What kind of a job?" Tyler asked.

"Developing new programs like this for the camp," Becca said slowly. "He says I could impact thousands of kids."

For a few moments the only sound in the lodge was the crackling of the fire.

"What are you going to tell him?" Solana finally asked.

Becca could almost feel the air pressure drop as her friends held their breath. "The only thing I can tell him," she said. She smiled and gave Nate the ghost of a wink before turning back to Solana. "No thanks."

life

love

Want More? Life
Go from ordinary to extraordinary! *Want More? Life* will help you open the door to God's abundant life. You'll go deeper, wider and higher in your walk with God in the midst of everyday challenges like self-image, guys, friendships and big decisions. Spiral hardcover.

Want More? Love
You may ask, "Does God really love me? How can He love me — with all my faults and flaws?" *Want More? Love* is a powerful devotional that shows you how passionately and protectively God loves and cares for you — and how you can love Him in return! Spiral hardcover.

Bloom: A Girl's Guide to Growing Up

You have lots of questions about life. In *Bloom: A Girl's Guide To Growing Up*, your questions are addressed and answered with the honesty youth expect and demand. From changing bodies, to dating and sex, to relationships, money and more, girls will find the answers they need. Paperback.

Brio

It's the inside scoop — with hot tips on everything from fashion and fitness to real-life faith. Monthly magazine.